Don't

Judge a

by Her

COVER

ally carter

SCHOLASTIC INC.
New York Toronto London Auckland
Sydney Mexico City New Delhi Hong Kong

ISBN 978-0-545-28433-2

12 11 10 9 8 7 6 5 4 3 2   10 11 12 13 14 15/0

Printed in the U.S.A.   40

First Scholastic Book Clubs printing, September 2010

This book is set in Goudy.

For Donna Bray,

the Gallagher Girl who started it all

Chapter One

"We're moving." The man beside me spoke into the microphone in his sleeve, and I knew the words weren't for me.

The August air was hot and thick with the smell of sea salt and bus exhaust. The roads were packed for miles, and everywhere I looked I saw shades of red, white, and blue. Everywhere I turned, I felt the eyes of trained professionals staring, seeing, recording every word, analyzing every glance within a dozen miles.

Part of me wanted to break free of the big men in the dark suits who flanked me on either side; another part wanted to marvel at the bomb-sniffing dogs who were examining boxes twenty meters away. But most of all, I wanted to lie when another man, with a clipboard and an earpiece, asked for my name.

After all, I've spent a lot of time learning how to whip out false IDs and recite perfectly crafted cover stories in situations just like these, so it was harder than I thought

1

to say, "Cammie. Cammie Morgan."

It was weirder than I would have guessed as I waited for him to scan *the clipboard and say,* "You can go right in."

As if I were simply a sixteen-year-old girl.

As if I couldn't possibly be a threat.

As if I didn't go to a school for spies.

Walking through the hotel lobby, I couldn't help but remember the first assignment my covert operations teacher ever gave me: *Notice things.* Lights and cameras shone from every angle. A massive net full of red, white, and blue balloons snaked through the cavernous space like a patriotic python. Up on the mezzanine level, the Texas delegation was singing about yellow roses, while a woman walked by wearing a big foam hat shaped like a Georgia peach.

I scanned the masses of old women and young girls. Husbands and wives. College kids and senior citizens. The last time I'd been in a crowd like this was in a different season and a different city, so maybe it was the hotel's frigid air-conditioning or just a memory of a chilly day in D.C., but for some reason, I shivered and fought against a serious case of déjà vu as I looked around and said the name I hadn't spoken in weeks. "Zach."

Then I blinked and wondered if a part of me would always worry that he might be on my tail.

"This way," the man beside me said, but we didn't stop at the end of the line, which twisted and turned in front of the marble-covered registration desk. We didn't even slow down as we passed between two rows of elevators. Instead we turned down a narrow hall that seemed half a world away from the bright lights and tall ceiling of the lobby. Plush carpeting gave way to chipped linoleum tiles until finally we were standing before an elevator I'm pretty sure hotel guests were never intended to see.

"So, you're a friend of peacocks?" the Secret Service agent asked while we waited for the doors to open.

"Excuse me?" I asked, because even though I'd never been in a really nice hotel, I was pretty sure they wouldn't have exotic birds on the penthouse level.

"Peacock," the agent said again as we stepped into the service car that was soon carrying us, nonstop, to the top floor. "See, we use code names," he explained as if I were . . . a sixteen-year-old girl, "when we talk about the protectee. So you and Peacock, you're . . . *friends?*" he asked, and again I realized that he wasn't looking at me the way a well-trained, well-armed security professional looks at a potential threat (because I know a thing or two about well-trained and well-armed security professionals!). Nope. He was looking at me like I was . . . a Gallagher Girl.

Of course, if you're reading this you must already know that there are two types of people in this world—those who know the truth about what goes on inside the walls of the Gallagher Academy for Exceptional Young Women, and those who don't. Something in the way the agent was trying to weigh my slightly out-of-style clothes against the snooty reputation of my school told me that he was definitely the second type—that he assumed we were all rich; that he thought we were all spoiled; and that he had no idea what it *really* meant to be Gallagher Girl.

And that was *before* I heard the screaming.

As the elevator doors slid open, a high-pitched "I am going to kill someone!" echoed from behind the double doors at the end of the hall.

And then I was one hundred percent certain that the man beside me didn't know the truth about my sisterhood, because he didn't draw his weapon; he didn't even flinch as a second Secret Service agent opened the double doors and whispered, "Peacock is angry."

Instead, he walked *toward* the screaming girl—even though she was a Gallagher Girl.

Even though her name was Macey McHenry.

Before that day, I'd never been to Boston. I'd never had a Secret Service escort. And I'd definitely never been a VIP (or the friend/roommate/guest of a VIP) at a national political convention. But walking into what I'm pretty sure was the hotel's second-nicest suite, I added another first to the list: I'd never seen Macey McHenry as mad as she was then.

"Really, Macey, I think it's an adorable little puff piece." Cynthia McHenry's cool, mannered tone could not have been more different from her daughter's. "He's the only son of a future president. . . . You're the only daughter of a future vice president. . . . If people want to read about the possibility of a White House wedding eight years from now, I don't see any reason to stop them. Really, I don't know why you have to be so dramatic."

4

Right then I made a mental note that if Mrs. McHenry thought Macey was too dramatic then she should probably never be left alone with the better part of our junior class.

"If that boy—"

"*That boy*," her mother corrected, "is Governor Winters's son—"

"—tries to flirt with me—" Macey went on, but Mrs. McHenry talked over her.

"And if appearing with that boy is going to give us a two-percent bump in Ohio, then you *will* appear with that boy."

"Percentages." Macey gave an exasperated sigh. "You know I don't do math."

Well, I have personally seen Macey McHenry do linear algebra without a calculator (after mastering our roommate Liz's system, of course), but the girl in front of me wasn't the Macey I knew from school. She wasn't the girl on the suite's TV either, smiling and waving and holding hands with her father on the national news. Instead she was the *other* kind of Gallagher Girl—the kind the agent had been expecting: the snobby kind, the spoiled kind, the kind who had crawled out of her parents' limousine and into our school nearly a year before with combat boots and a diamond nose stud.

"This was the scene this morning as Senator James McHenry and his family arrived here in Boston to join Governor Winters and officially accept the vice presidential nomination," the TV anchor was saying. But I doubt that Macey or her mother were even listening as they stared daggers at each other.

"You will do this, Macey," her mother said. "You will—"

But then my escort cleared his throat, and Mrs. McHenry turned. I expected her to gush like she had on the phone when Macey had called to invite me to join them, but instead she waved in my direction and said, "There, your little friend is here."

Something in the way her mother spoke about me made Macey draw a breath. I was relieved that no one else noticed how my roommate's fists clenched tighter for just a moment before she spun around and snapped, "We're going for a walk."

"Don't forget the rehearsal!" her mother called, but Macey was already pulling me through the double doors.

I caught the agent's eye one final time as he tried to figure out what I could possibly have in common with the girl who was pulling me along. On the TV, someone said, "Cynthia McHenry is a well-known businesswoman and philanthropist. The couple has one daughter, Macey, a student at the Gallagher Academy for Exceptional Young Women, in Roseville, Virginia."

Our school.

National television.

A thousand thoughts raced through my mind before Macey slammed the doors behind us, as if trapping my worries on the other side. She smiled a mischievous smile, and for the first time that day I recognized my friend in the girl who stood before me. "So, how do you like my cover?"

Chapter two

Spies have covers for every occasion: aliases and phony passports, pocket litter and fake IDs. A great operative can become someone else at the drop of a hat (and sometimes, actual hats are involved), but I'd rarely seen someone as deeply undercover as Macey McHenry was then.

"Peacock is moving," one of the agents whispered into his cuff as I followed Macey through the Winters-McHenry temporary headquarters, past rows of laptop computers and screaming interns wearing business suits and campaign buttons and looking like they hadn't had a good night's sleep since New Hampshire. In fact, I actually heard one guy say, "I haven't had a good night's sleep since New Hampshire."

But Macey's black hair was as glossy as ever, her blue eyes perfectly clear. "Jeez, Chameleon, do you have any idea how hard you are to track down?" She walked on, seemingly unaware that she was like a princess, and the room was full of commoners who were there to make sure her father claimed his throne. "I mean, first I tried the school, but have you ever tried to get anything out of Professor Buckingham?" My roommate calmly rattled on as if her face weren't being broadcast into every home in America at that very moment. "Anyway, then I asked the Secret Service, and—"

"Wait," I interrupted. "The Secret Service gave you my grandparents' telephone number?"

"Well," Macey admitted, "I asked the Secret Service for the number, but I ended up getting it from more *covert* sources."

I lowered my voice when I asked, "The agency?"

"Liz," she whispered back, and I couldn't help smile as I thought about our tiniest/smartest roommate. "So, have a good summer?" Macey asked as we left the war room and started down another long hall.

"Yeah," I said, almost out of breath. Two months at my grandparents' ranch in Nebraska hadn't made me completely out of shape, but life moved at a different pace there, so it still felt like a struggle to keep up with Macey. "It was good. Just . . ."

I thought about our classmates, who seemed to scatter to the far corners of the world whenever school wasn't in session. I thought about my mother, who had put me on a plane the first day of summer break and hadn't sent so much as a postcard since. And finally, I thought about two boys: one who I hadn't seen in months and one who I seemed to be imagining everywhere, but whom I knew I might never see again.

"Fine," I said finally. "My summer was fine."

Macey knew me pretty well by then, so she just smiled and said, "Mine too."

Our footsteps were whisper-soft against the carpeting as we entered the tunnel that passed under the street between the convention center and the hotel.

Secret Service agents flanked the doors, and I heard one whisper into his sleeve, "Peacock is arriving on the scene."

"So can *I* call you Peacock?" I teased.

"That depends: do you want to feel safe while you sleep at . . ." Macey started, but then two elderly women wearing the biggest sunflowers I have ever seen passed us, and Macey smiled at them—yes, actual *smileage*—and said, "Well, doesn't the Kansas delegation look festive!"

The shift in her had been effortless, as if her thousand-watt smile was attached to a switch that the fates kept flipping off and on. Sure, I might have been the CIA legacy, but right then it was obvious that Macey knew as much about secret identities, hidden agendas, and covert alliances as anyone I'd ever known.

"So," I started, "what's new with you?"

She pulled a neatly typed piece of paper from her pocket. "Six a.m.: appear on national morning shows. Nine a.m.: get fitted for navy suits." Macey leaned closer and added in a whisper, "Evidently, red makes me look trampy." She resumed her usual posture and walked faster, the sloping ramp leading us closer and closer to a pair of metal doors at the end of the tunnel. "Eleven a.m.," she continued, "fun, family bonding with Mom and Dad."

Macey stopped. She rested her hands on the metal handles.

"So, you know," she said as she pushed open the doors of the single largest room I've ever seen, "the usual."

Chairs—thousands of empty chairs—spread across the arena floor. Signs bearing the names of all the states hung above them. We started out in Oregon, then walked through Delaware and past Kentucky. Stands rose high before us. I craned my head upward, scanning the skyboxes that circled the arena, boasting the logos of every news outlet known to man.

Macey and I stood there for a long moment, alone for the first time. Maybe that's why she felt safe to whisper, "Thanks for coming, Cam."

Her father's face was on the cover of every magazine in America. She was about to be the belle of the country's biggest ball. Probably every girl in the country would have traded places with her, but I saw the misery in her eyes as she stood lost inside that massive space, and I knew why I was there. I remembered that a Gallagher Girl is only as good as her backup.

"Let's get this over with and get back to school, okay?" I said.

"Okay," she replied. I could have sworn she almost smiled.

And she might have if we hadn't been interrupted by the sound of footsteps from behind us and a voice saying, "Hello, ladies."

I don't know about you, but there are certain assumptions I tend to make about a teenage boy who insists on calling teenage girls "ladies." You expect him to be handsome. You expect him to be slick. The kind of guy who owns more hair styling products than you do.

But Preston Winters was . . . not.

He was about Macey's height, but I don't think I'm exaggerating when I say I'm pretty sure Liz could have taken him in a fistfight. His tailored suit hung from his thin frame like he was a kid playing dress-up, which wasn't much of a stretch considering the fact that he was wearing a Spider-Man wristwatch.

"Quick question," Macey whispered. "When your mom said that we weren't supposed to use any Protection and Enforcement moves this summer, that didn't apply to presidential candidates' sons, did it?"

"I think it might apply *especially* to them."

I'm not sure if it was the presence of the Secret Service or the classified nature of our sisterhood, but something made Macey take a deep breath and smile (and whisper a really bad word in Portuguese).

"You're looking very . . . patriotic . . . today, Ms. McHenry," Preston said, looking Macey up and down.

I glanced at Macey's red, white, and blue sweater set (I

know . . . *Macey* was wearing a *sweater set*!) and bit back a laugh.

"I don't believe we've met," the boy said, turning to me and holding out his hand. "I'm Preston. You must be—"

"Busy," Macey said, trying to pull me away.

"Cammie," I finished, resisting my roommate's pull long enough to shake Preston's hand. "The roommate," I offered.

He bowed slightly forward at the waist and said, "It's nice to meet you, Cammie the roommate—"

Before he could finish I heard a shrill voice cry, "McHenry family, stage left!" A trim woman was walking onto the stage, Macey's mom and dad following closely behind her. She had a clipboard. And little horn-rimmed glasses hanging from a chain around her neck. And not one but two pencils stuck in the massive pile of hair on the top of her head.

"Winters family, stage right!"

As the governor of Vermont and his wife took their places, I couldn't help but notice that one of the most powerful men in the country looked absolutely terrified of the woman with the clipboard.

"McHenry family!" the woman called again. "We're missing—"

"Here I am," Macey said, dashing toward the stage.

Her mother rolled her eyes. Her father checked his watch. But Clipboard Lady just said, "Excellent! We can't have a new Camelot without our young people. Just look at those bright shiny faces."

"Actually, I owe my complexion to your company, Mrs. McHenry." The entire group seemed surprised to hear Preston speaking—especially Preston. But instead of shutting up, he rambled on. "That new blemish reduction cream is . . . wow. Good job," he added with a self-conscious nod. Clipboard Lady glared at him, and it was pretty obvious that the shining faces were supposed to be seen and not heard. "I'll be standing over here now," Preston said, taking his place beside his parents.

The candidates took turns behind a podium draped with what looked like every red, white, and blue piece of fabric east of the Mississippi. Macey stayed in the center of it all, never shrinking from the spotlight, while I eased to the back of the arena and took my place among the shadows.

Number of times Clipboard Lady made Governor Winters and Macey's dad practice shaking hands and then turn to wave at the imaginary crowd: 14

Number of times Macey glared at her mother: 26

Number of times Preston tried to catch Macey's attention and she totally ignored him: 27

Number of times Macey had to practice a "spontaneous" dip while dancing with her father: 5

Number of minutes I had to sit alone in that enormous arena, wondering if freedom and democracy were always this well rehearsed: 55

By noon, Clipboard Lady was running through things one final time.

"At exactly 8:04 the music will come up." Clipboard Lady raised her hands dramatically. "At this point," she said, studying the candidates and their families over her dark-rimmed glasses, "I recommend spontaneous dancing."

Preston smiled at Macey. Macey shuddered.

"Balloons will fall at 8:06. Celebrate, celebrate. Dance, dance. Fade to commercial."

"All done?" I asked when Macey appeared beside me a minute later. She looked more relieved than I've ever seen her. (And that's including the time Dr. Fibs announced that he wouldn't be needing her to help him with his bunion-pads-as-weapons experiment. Which, needless to say, is pretty darn relieved.)

"Let's go," Macey told me, but we both must have gotten a little bit sloppy over summer vacation, because Preston was already on our tail.

"So, can I interest you ladies in some midday refreshment? I hear the Hawaii delegation might be roasting a big pig." At that point I might have felt sorry for Preston because that was maybe the dorkiest thing I'd ever heard. But Preston didn't shy away from his dorkiness—he *embraced* it. No part of Preston Winters felt sorry for himself. He was the only person I'd ever met who was completely without a cover. And I liked him for it.

"Sorry, Preston," Macey said as she grabbed my arm and pointed me toward the doors. She waved her well-worn itinerary in front of him. "Duty calls."

But if there's one thing that living with the child of a career politician has taught me, it's that they never take no for an answer.

"Hey," he said. "Yeah. Itineraries. Doing our part. That's great." We were ten steps ahead of him, but for a skinny guy he was really pretty fast. And persistent. "I'll walk with."

Since there were two Secret Service agents flanking us, and a news crew setting up for a live feed, Macey must have thought twice about stopping him. Instead she pushed against the metal doors again, and soon we were retracing our steps through the underground tunnel.

An older man with crazy white hair and wild eyebrows nearly ran me over, mumbling a very southern, "Excuse me, miss." A pair of women wearing "Washingtonians for Winters" T-shirts practically bowed in front of Preston, but he just kept pace beside us, almost jogging to keep up.

"So, you ladies go to the same school, I take it?" Preston gasped. "Are all the women of the Gallagher Academy as striking as the two of you?"

Macey spun on him. "Actually, striking is what we do best."

"So, Preston," I said, eager to change the subject. We turned down the dingy narrow corridor that had taken me to Macey that morning. "You must be excited . . . about your dad. First son. All that."

"Oh, yeah," Preston said. "I'm very excited about my father's plan for America."

He might have been a politician's son, but I was a spy's daughter, so I knew a lie when I heard one. As we reached the service elevator, I watched Macey frantically punch the button, saw her mentally planning ways to keep Preston out, but all I could do was think about another boy and another elevator, and remember that there are some things even a Gallagher Girl can't keep from sneaking up on her.

As the doors slid open, we all climbed on. It was tight fit, so one of the Secret Service agents held back.

"This is Charlie, by the way," Preston said, gesturing to the man who seemed to take up more than his fair share of the small space. "Charlie's been with me since . . . when was it? Missouri, I think?"

The door slid closed. Charlie didn't say a word. And beneath his breath, I heard Preston fill the awkward silence with a whisper, "Good times."

The ride to the top seemed slightly longer this time. I should have wondered why, but I didn't—not until I heard the ding and saw the doors slide open onto a space that I was certain I had never seen before.

We might as well have been in a different country—much less a different building—as we stepped into the fluorescent glare of a room that had no red carpets, no rushing interns or patient guards. A room-service cart that was missing two wheels sat along one wall. There were laundry carts and old headboards. Massive machines churned, filling the space with loud noise and an almost unbearable heat.

"Did you hit the wrong button?" I asked, looking at Macey.

"It says 12:05: film promotional video. Service elevator. Level R." She pointed to the big R that had been painted on the wall in front of us.

I glanced at Charlie, who hadn't said a word since we left the convention center floor, but he didn't hesitate to hold up his sleeve and say, "Control, I'm with Peacock and Mad Dog—"

Beside me, Preston raised his eyebrows and whispered, "I picked that myself."

But Charlie carried on. "We're on Level R. Are they filming the video here, or has that been changed?" He looked at me. "They're checking."

The air was hot and stale, the room way too small to be an entire floor. A door with a small window was at the far end, so I wasn't surprised to hear Macey say, "I bet we're supposed to be out here," and see her push out into the light.

There are many things a Gallagher Girl has to be: adventurous, daring, and totally unafraid of heights, to name a few. And all of those came in handy as Macey, Preston, and I stepped out onto the hotel's roof.

A strong wind blew off the harbor, banging the metal door shut behind us. As we stepped toward the roof's edge and peered out across the city, we saw historic church steeples and towering skyscrapers. Some buildings looked as if Paul Revere himself were going to step outside; others seemed straight out of the future. Sixty stories below, news vans and tour busses stood on the gridlocked highways, but on the hotel's roof the chaos of the convention seemed to be far, far away. And that, I guess, was the problem.

There were no camera crews, no public relations specialists. I glanced at Macey, who said what I was thinking. "This isn't right." Then she turned to Preston. "Where were we supposed to be, exactly?" Macey looked from Preston to her well-worn agenda, and then she finally held out her hand. "Let me see *your* itinerary."

"Okay, yeah . . . see that's not so easy to . . ." Preston stumbled for words and then admitted, "My mom has it."

I looked behind us, searching for Charlie, but the man was nowhere to be seen, and in that moment, everything seemed to change.

Maybe it was my four full years of training, or my sixteen-and-a-half years of being Rachel Morgan's daughter, but somehow, some way, I knew that rooftop was a very bad place to be.

"Hey, you're"—Preston started as I ran toward the heavy metal door—"a really fast runner."

But I barely heard him as I pulled with all my might against the door, trying the handle in vain, banging against the gray metal. It was locked—or jammed—and there was no leaving the way we'd come.

"This isn't right," Macey said behind me, double-checking her itinerary, still so entrenched in the part of herself that was a politician's daughter that she was ignoring the other part—the spy part—the girl she thought she wouldn't get to be during her summer vacation.

"Something's just not . . ." but then she trailed off. Macey's blue eyes stared into mine. I saw in them a realization—a fear—as she looked down at the paper in her hands and then back at me. . . .

And then toward the helicopter that was flying too low, too fast, and heading right for us.

Chapter tHReE

Here's the thing about covert operations: the really bad things always happen when you least expect them. The bad guys don't give you a heads-up when you're going to be attacked. They don't let you wait thirty minutes after eating. And they never, ever let you stop to put on comfortable shoes.

So training for that kind of life means one thing: spy school is never really out of session.

I thought about the piece of paper in Macey's hands and told myself that it could have been an innocent mistake, a change of plans. It didn't mean that our teachers had intentionally drawn Macey—and by extension, me—onto a roof with some kind of terrible test in mind. It didn't mean we had a fight coming. It didn't mean my heart had reason to race.

But still I looked at my roommate and asked, "Are you thinking what I'm thinking?"

Macey shrugged. "Our teachers wouldn't do anything in

front of him." She gestured to Preston, who was leaning over the railing, staring down at the chaos on the street below, completely oblivious to the dark spot that was on the horizon and moving in fast.

I thought about Preston's missing itinerary. "Maybe he wasn't supposed to be here?"

And with that, Macey let her piece of paper fall; I saw it flit and float in the air, and swirl around us as the chopper hovered lower. It was as if Macey had let her cover fall as well. The hotel was full of people who would only see the candidate's daughter, but right then—right there—there was no doubt who Macey McHenry had to be.

"Hey, you guys, look at—" Preston said, finally noticing the helicopter above us. He stopped suddenly as a rope fell from the chopper and dangled between sky and roof.

I heard a click, a metallic creak as the door to the roof opened. But instead of Charlie, two masked figures stepped into the glaring sun. And then I couldn't help myself; I screamed, "I'm on summer vacation!"

I felt Macey at my back, saw Preston staring at a dark figure rappelling from the helicopter as if he'd somehow stumbled into a video game—or a nightmare. "They don't look like undecided voters," he said, as if sarcasm were a weapon he'd relied on his entire life and he really didn't want it to fail him then.

The masked figures didn't rush toward us. They weren't sloppy. They were deliberate. They were good, moving with purpose, keeping an even spacing as Macey and I stood back-to-back, bracing ourselves in the center of the roof.

"Preston!" I yelled. "Get down!"

I wanted him to hide. I wanted him to be unconscious or blind. I wanted him anywhere but there. I already knew too well how having a civilian boy in the middle of a CoveOps exercise can turn out. It was a chapter I didn't need to read again.

"This isn't"—I said with a grunt as I parried the attacker's first blow—"a very"—I took a half-step to my right and landed a kick at one of the masked men's knees—"good time for me!"

A masked man stood in front of me. Blazing white teeth shone behind his dark mask. For a split second I thought it was the smile of Mr. Solomon. The first attacker who had come from the chopper had the unmistakable curves of a beautiful woman, and a part of me wondered if it was my mom.

But then from nowhere I felt a punch in my side, a perfect blow, and as I fell onto the sticky tar-covered roof, I saw news choppers beginning to swoop and swarm around us—and I knew.

I knew no one at the Gallagher Academy would be this careless.

I knew my mother and Mr. Solomon would rather die than risk exposure of our school on this kind of stage.

I knew there was something more behind the punch—not in the attacker's fist, but in his eyes.

And then, more than ever, I knew I had to get Macey and Preston off the roof.

I don't know how to explain what happened next, but in that instant, all the P&E lessons I'd ever had came back to me. In that moment, I knew surviving wasn't just about punches and kicks; it's about geometry and it's about timing; it's about having your reflexes speed up while your mind slows down.

Maybe it lasted a minute; maybe it lasted a month. All I really know for sure is that one of the men moved toward me. I ducked as his fist flew, narrowly missing my head, and yet my focus was already somewhere else—my eyes were scanning the roof, looking for a weapon, a way out, or both. And that's when I saw it—a narrow window washer's plank dangling off the side of the roof. It had rails on both sides and was attached to a pulley system.

My heart pounded. The wind roared in my ears as I grabbed Preston's hand and screamed, "Come on!"

There were footsteps behind me—a hand on my arm. I spun around, but before I could land a blow, Preston pulled back his free hand and punched the man in the throat. It was a perfect lucky shot, but I was willing to take any help I could get as I pulled the potential first son out of harm's way and onto the narrow plank.

"I hit a guy," Preston said, staring at his fist as if *that* were the most shocking thing of all.

"I know. Good job," I said, reaching for the controls; but then for the first time Preston seemed to notice that I had guided him onto something that was dangling off the side of a sixty-story-building.

"Wait!" he shouted.

"You'll be fine," I told him.

"But shouldn't I . . ." he muttered in the manner of a boy who knows he should be chivalrous but doesn't quite know how.

Behind me, I heard Macey cry out in pain, but I kept my focus and hit the green button, knowing somehow that getting Preston off that roof was my mission at that moment.

"Hang on!" I yelled, and in the next instant gravity took over and Preston dropped twenty stories to safety.

I might have savored that fact, but the attackers seemed to refocus, and I watched the woman raise her hand and point to where Macey was taking her place by my side.

"Get her," the woman ordered. I stole a sideways glance at my friend, the daughter of a United States senator and one of the wealthiest women in the world. My friend, who had been featured on every newsstand in America. My friend, who would be any kidnapper's dream.

Macey and I were retreating slowly, coming closer and closer to the wall behind us, and I knew we were cornered.

"No," I cried, as if that was all it would take for them to stop.

And then I saw it—a rusty vent ten feet to the right of the door I'd given up any hope of opening. I dropped to the ground, kicked the vent as hard as I could, and felt it give slightly. I kicked again while, behind me, the men lunged for Macey. I heard a sickening snap. I turned and saw my roommate clutch her arm and fall to the ground, howling out in pain, so I kicked harder, and this time the old vent buckled under the pressure. It popped free, and I hurled it toward the head of one of the men who was reaching for Macey. I heard the crash of metal against skull, but I didn't stop to survey the damage—I was too busy grabbing Macey and pushing her toward the hole in the wall that the vent had left.

I started to follow, but someone grasped my shoulders with a steel grip holding me to the spot. I clawed against her; but as I tried to pry myself free, my hand brushed against a gold ring engraved with an emblem that I could have sworn I'd seen before. For a split second my mind went still as I tried to place it, but then I heard a frail voice say "Cam," and I remembered my friend—my mission.

I clawed harder, leaning forward, praying that my momentum would take me through the gap in the wall to a safer place. Suddenly, I remembered the Winters McHenry campaign button on my blouse. I heard my shirt rip as I pulled the button free and jabbed the pin into the hand on my left shoulder.

The woman behind me howled in pain as I pushed Macey all the way through the vent and followed after her.

"Run, Macey!" I screamed. "Go!"

I wasn't thinking. No strategies came to mind. No flash cards. No vocabulary words. It was the age-old case of fight versus flight. I looked at Macey, whose arm hung at a strange angle; I felt my side and knew my ribs were bruised at best and maybe broken, and I knew that fight wouldn't be an option much longer—that we had to get out of there and soon.

"Go," I told her. Behind us, I heard the metal door open again. A flash of light sliced across the cement floor, illuminating a pair of long legs bent at an odd angle, protruding from behind one of the room's massive machines.

I heard Macey whisper, "Charlie."

We pushed past the churning machines and skirted a decade's worth of broken furniture and hotel relics until we reached the elevator that had brought us there.

And then for the first time, I honestly felt like I could cry.

The elevator's doors stood open. Mangled wires protruded from the control box, still sparking where they'd been pulled out of the wall and sliced in two with professional precision.

There was no place we could run. No place we could hide. I turned to look at the three figures, approaching us in perfect formation—a hunting party with a helicopter ready to take my friend to someplace I didn't dare imagine.

I glanced around for a weapon, found a rolling cart and pushed it toward them with all my might, hoping it might serve as the greatest bowling ball in history and knock the black-clad figures down in one swipe. But the man in front merely tossed it aside.

"Cam," Macey whispered. She was growing paler. Her left arm had swollen to twice its normal size, but still she managed to point with her right toward a square hole in the wall—a shaft or chute of some kind.

I didn't know what it was or where it led. And I didn't have time to ask. I just dove, pushing Macey ahead of me.

One of the men lunged forward. I heard a cry of "no" reverberating down the shaft, but it was too late. Gravity had taken over, and I was hurtling toward the unknown, praying that it would be better than the place I had just left.

Free-falling, I felt my head bang against the metal shaft. Something hot and wet oozed into my eyes, and still I felt . . . grateful . . . hopeful. Dizzy.

There was a soft thump. The ground beneath me seemed to roll, but at least there was ground.

I turned and squinted through dizziness and pain to see a red drop fall onto white sheets. Macey lay unconscious beside me.

I lay my head back and felt the world begin to spin. In the distance, someone yelled, "United States Secret Service, open up!"

And through a hazy fog, my mind drifted back to the last time the world had gone upside down. A boy was dipping me in the center of my school and kissing me. For a moment, I could almost see his face leaning toward me, as if my life were flashing before my eyes.

And then the whole world faded to black.

Chapter foUR

Not all sleep is equal, of that much I am sure. After all, I've experienced many varieties of it firsthand. There's Bex-challenged-me-to-a-round-of-kickboxing sleep, where exhaustion is matched only by the aching of your body. There's Grandma-Morgan-made-a-huge-dinner-and-there's-nowhere-I-have-to-be-for-three-weeks sleep that only comes in places where you feel utterly safe. And then there's the other kind—the worst kind—when your body goes someplace your mind can't follow: the Mom-just-told-me-Dad's-never-coming-home-again sleep. Your body rests, but your heart . . . it has other things to do, and you wake up the next morning praying, hoping, willing the night before to have been a terrible dream.

I'd never known it was possible to have all three kinds at once. But it is. I know that now.

"Don't move," a deep voice said.

I felt the light first, burning through my closed eyes,

forcing me to turn my head away from the glare. As I moved, a rush of white-hot pain seared through me, and a deep voice chuckled.

"I know you're not big on following rules, Ms. Morgan, but when I tell you to stay still, you might want to do as I say."

I blinked and swallowed, but my mouth felt as if it were full of sand, my eyes like burning embers. I tried to sit upright, but a hand eased me back down onto soft pillows. I looked up at the blurry face of my mother—my headmistress—and the best spy I've ever known.

And then somehow I found the strength to say, "That wasn't a test, was it?"

I didn't know where I was, or even the day or the time, but I knew my mother's face, and that was enough to tell me the answer to my question.

"Welcome back," I heard the deep voice say, and I turned to see Joe Solomon standing at the foot of my bed; but for the first time since I'd met him, I wasn't worried about what my hair looked like in his presence.

"Mr.—" I started, my voice rough.

"Here." My mother brought a glass of water to my lips, but I couldn't drink.

"Macey," I cried, sitting up too quickly. My head swam and my throat burned, but nothing could stop me. A thousand questions came to mind, but right then only one really mattered. "Macey! Is she—"

"She's fine," Mom said soothingly.

"Better than you, actually," Mr. Solomon said. "A broken arm isn't quite as scary as . . ." He trailed off but tapped his temple, and for the first time I felt the bandage that covered my head. I remembered the fall through the shaft, the blood in my eyes, and then, spy training or not, I felt a little woozy and lay back down on the pillow.

"Where am I?" I asked, noticing that instead of the skirt I'd been wearing in Boston, I had on my oldest and softest pair of pajamas. Instead of the soreness of fresh bruises, my body ached as if I hadn't moved in years, so then I knew to modify my question. "*When* am I?"

"You've been out for a little more than a day," Mr. Solomon said. "We brought you here as soon as we could."

"Here?" I looked around. The log wall beside my bed was rough beneath my fingers. The floors were solid wood. I was in a cabin, I realized, probably belonging to the school or the CIA. "Is this a safe house?"

I didn't have a clue *how* safe it was until I heard my teacher say, "It had better be. I own it."

Mr. Solomon owned a house. Mr. Solomon owned *this* house. On any other day I might have absorbed every detail of the place—the patchwork quilt, the tackle box, the smell of fresh pine and old mothballs. I might have marveled that Mr. Solomon *lived* anywhere, that he had roots.

"I don't use it much," Mr. Solomon said, as if reading my mind. "But it has come in handy"—he seemed to be considering his words—"on occasion."

I didn't stop to think about the "occasions" of Mr. Solomon's life. I knew my imagination could never do them justice, so instead I just sat there trying to summon the courage to say, "Charlie?"

Mom smiled. She smoothed my hair. "He's going to make it, Cam. He's going to be fine."

It should have calmed me, but it didn't. The sun broke through the heavy trees outside, and rays fell across the bed. I sat up a little straighter. "Is Macey here too?"

My teacher nodded. "Outside. It took a little doing to get her away from the Secret Service after everything, but"— he trailed off, glanced at my mother then back to me— "we've done harder."

Sometimes it seems like we Gallagher Girls spend half our time wondering about the things that our teachers have seen and done. But that day I didn't ask for details. That day, I had seen enough to know that maybe I didn't want to hear the stories.

"What happened?" I asked. I didn't look at my mother or my teacher. My fingers traced the pattern of the quilt. I was the one who had been there, and yet all I could do was say, "I mean, was it . . ."

"A kidnapping attempt?" Mr. Solomon finished for me, and I nodded, trying to act as professional as my teacher sounded. "These things, they happen—or almost happen— more than you'd think." I tried to nod and smile. After all, the true measure of covert operations lies in how much nobody ever knows. But people were going to know about this. "Ninety-nine times out of a hundred it doesn't get that far, but—"

"They were good," I said, almost shaking with the memory.

Mr. Solomon nodded. "Yeah," he said, as if a part of him couldn't help but be impressed. "They were. Secret Service and FBI are going to have some questions for you. Ms. Morgan, these agents will have Level Six clearance at the most—so you know what you're going to have to tell them?"

I nodded. "My roommate invited me to the convention. We were attacked on the roof. We got away." I felt myself reciting the cover story I'd have to tell; I found myself remembering that I know fourteen different languages and yet my life is ruled by the things I cannot say.

I glanced out the window, saw the trees that surrounded us, a clearing, and in the distance a sparkling lake. Macey stood on the end of a long pier, looking out at the water.

"We got lucky," I added softly, and at that moment my cover story didn't feel like a lie at all.

My mother's cell phone rang and she rushed to take it. I heard her whispering to someone she called Sir. I turned and looked out the window at the girl on the pier, and then I got up slowly and stepped toward an old-fashioned screened door.

"There's nothing wrong up there," Mr. Solomon said. I stopped and turned to see him pointing toward my groggy head. "Trust me, Cammie, everything's gonna be fine." He touched a faded scar on his temple. "I know a little something about these things."

Mr. Solomon was the best teacher I'd ever had, and I didn't want to disappoint him. So I lied and said, "I know."

"Hey," I said as I reached the end of the pier. Macey was still standing there, staring out at the still, quiet lake. Scrapes ran down her left cheek. Her right eye was rimmed with black, and her left arm dangled from a totally unflattering sling. As I walked toward her, I couldn't help but think that if that was what *Macey* looked like, then I probably never wanted to see a mirror again.

"Welcome back," she said.

"Thanks."

"How's the head?"

"Hurts. How's the arm?" My roommate didn't answer. She didn't comment on my hideous hair or the bruises on our faces that no amount of concealer could hide.

There were too many things to say, so I didn't press her. Instead I shifted and listened to the boards creak beneath my feet and thought about how our school had taught us how to get off that roof, but nothing in our exceptional education had told us what we were supposed to do next.

I wanted to sit in the CoveOps classroom and listen while Mr. Solomon dissected every move, every clue, every punch.

And I wanted to block it from my mind and never think about it again.

I wanted to know who had done this and why and how.

And I wanted to believe that it was over, and those

were the kinds of details that didn't matter now.

I wanted to take the greatest training I had ever received and learn from it, and be better because of it.

And I wanted it to stop being real.

I wanted a thousand different things as we stood there, but most of all, I wanted the girl who had been beside me in Boston to turn and realize that I was beside her now.

"I heard Charlie is going to make it," I said, but Macey didn't smile.

"Have you talked to Preston?" I tried, but her gaze never wavered.

"Macey, do you want to talk about it?" I asked, but her breathing stayed steady, her gaze didn't move.

"Macey," I tried, "please say something. Please say—"

"It's nice," she said as the late-summer breeze blew through the trees. "I like this. I like the water."

"Don't you have a house on Martha's Vineyard?" I asked, wondering how a rickety shack on a quiet lake could ever compare; but Macey kept staring at the stillness and said, "This is better."

"We're going to have to answer questions. We're going to have to be very careful about what we say. We're—"

"They briefed me already," Macey said, her eyes never leaving the horizon. "This *feels* like a safe house." She finally turned to look at me. "Doesn't it feel safe, Cam?"

"Yeah, Macey," I said softly. "It does."

It was getting late. My internal clock had rebooted, and something in the way the sun dipped behind the tree-covered hills that surrounded us on all sides told me it was nearly eight o'clock.

"It's almost time," Macey said as if she'd read my mind. "They're coming. My parents want me with them—"

"Of course," I blurted.

"—on the campaign trail," Macey finished. I stared at her, forgetting my aching head and sore muscles for a moment. She forced a smile. "We're up ten points in the polls."

I didn't know what to say, so I didn't say a thing. Instead, we stood there until we heard the screen door behind us screech and slam. A minute later a helicopter appeared on the horizon and dipped, its whirling blades sending ripples across the quiet lake before landing somewhere in the forest.

The wind grew cooler. Macey wrapped her good arm around herself and shivered in the breeze, but she didn't move from the end of the dock.

Her name was probably on every newscast in America. It wasn't hard to imagine that, back in Boston, a room full of interns was buzzing about speeches that had to be rewritten and commercials that had to be recut. The campaign had a new star—a new angle. But all of that felt like another world, so I just stood by my friend and thought for the first time ever that Joe Solomon was wrong about something.

I hadn't come away in worse shape than Macey McHenry.

Not by a long shot.

Chapter five

I know the sounds my school makes—the squeaky steps and creaking doors, the hushed voices during finals week, the noisy chaos of the Grand Hall before dinner. The first day of a new year has a sound all its own, as limos turn down the winding lane and car doors slam, suitcases bang against banisters, and girls squeal and hug hello.

But the first semester of my junior year . . . That semester started with a whisper so quiet I almost didn't hear it.

"Is Macey taking the semester off?" one senior asked another as they stood huddled in the hall outside the library.

"I heard they had to amputate Macey's arm and replace it with a bionic limb that Dr. Fibs made in his lab," an eighth grader said when I passed by the door to their common room.

Gallagher Girls spend their free time scattered throughout the four corners of the world, but that year every girl who returned from summer break brought back the same questions. So I kept moving, roaming the quiet halls like a shadow, right up until the point when I turned the corner and ran into Tina Walters.

"Cammie!" Tina cried, and in the newfound quiet of our school, the word echoed. She threw her arms around me. "You're okay!" she proclaimed, and then she reconsidered. "You are okay, aren't you?"

"Yeah, Tina, I'm—"

"Because I heard you killed one of them with a campaign button?"

Tina is a teenage girl, and a spy-in-training, and the only daughter of one of the country's premiere gossip columnists, so it's not surprising that she has crazy theories. A lot of them. All the time. But in that second, my mind flashed back to the sunny roof. I saw the shadows of the spinning blades, felt the hands that gripped my shoulders, and then heard the pained cry as I jabbed the Winters-McHenry button into a hand wearing a ring that I was sure I'd seen before.

"Cam?" Tina asked, but I just nodded.

"Yeah, Tina." My throat felt strange. as I said it. "Something like that."

And then I walked away.

When you're known as the Chameleon, sometimes it can feel like your whole life is just an elaborate game of hide-and-seek. Fortunately, I am very good at hiding. Unfortunately, my best friends are very good at seeking.

"Cam!" someone called through the shadows. "We know you're in here." The voice was soft and Southern, the footsteps so dainty that I knew there could only be one person tiny enough to creep over those particular floorboards without making a sound.

"Oh, Cammie," Liz practically sang, as she crept down the ancient corridor that (I think) had once been a pretty important part of the Underground Railroad, and had more recently served a far less noble covert purpose.

"I thought we'd find you here," another voice said. My second roommate pushed her way out of the shadows.

If possible, I think Liz had gotten even tinier and Bex had gotten even prettier over the summer break. Liz's blond hair was almost totally white from spending all summer in the sun. Bex's accent was stronger, like it always is after spending months with her parents in England. (Of course, Bex swore that she'd spent a good portion of that time actually doing surveillance with MI6 in an African nation that shall remain nameless.) Her dark skin glowed and her hair was longer than it had been at the start of the summer.

"Isn't it a tad early in the semester for hiding, darling?" Bex tried to tease. I tried to smile.

"What gave me away?" I asked.

"Irregular dust patterns outside the entrance," Bex said. "You're getting sloppy." And then she stopped. Strong Bex, brave Bex, seemed to recoil when she realized what she'd said. "I didn't mean . . ."

"It's okay, Bex," I told her.

"You *weren't* sloppy!" Bex blurted again.

Then Liz jumped in. "Everyone's talking about how

great you were—about how, if you hadn't been there . . ." But she didn't finish, which was just as well. No one wanted to think about how that sentence had to end.

Bex eased onto one of the overturned crates and boxes that filled the room. "Have you seen her?"

"Not since the day after. They brought us to Mr. Solomon's lake house, but then they took her back to her parents."

"She *is* coming back," Liz asked. "Isn't she?"

"I don't know," I said with a shrug.

"I mean . . . they wouldn't want her to stay with them all the time, would they? They'd want her here, where she's safe?"

"I don't know, Liz," I said, sharper than I'd meant. "I mean . . . I don't know if she's coming," I said, more softly. "I don't know who tried to do this or why or . . . I just don't know," I whispered again, then turned to look out the tiny circular window.

"She invited me." Bex's voice cut through the silence. "Before the convention, she called our flat and asked me to come, but my mum and dad were home, and I . . ." Bex trailed off, not knowing, I guess, that wanting to be with your parents isn't actually a sign of weakness. "I should have been there." She didn't sound envious about missing out on a good fight. Instead, she sounded guilty.

"Me too," Liz said, sinking to the dusty floor. "When she called, my mom said I could go, but I only had a few days left with my parents, so I said no."

I nodded. We all thought we'd have the better part of a

year to spend together, but in any life—especially a spy's life—tomorrow is never guaranteed.

And there you have it—the most important thing any of us had learned over our summer vacation.

"Tina Walters says Macey's parents have hired an ex-Navy SEAL to pose as a Sherpa and hide Macey out in the Himalayas until the election is over," Liz offered.

"Yeah, well Tina Walters says a lot of things. Tina Walters is usually wrong," Bex replied. But I thought about how close Tina had been with her campaign button theory; I remembered that Tina had been saying for years that there was an elite boys' school for spies, and we'd all thought that was a crazy rumor until last semester when a delegation from the Blackthorne Institute had moved into the East Wing, just a few feet from where we now sat.

So I looked around the empty dusty space and said, "Not always."

Last spring, finding out who those boys were and whether or not they could be trusted had seemed like the most important mission of our lives. Charts of surveillance summaries and patterns of behaviors still lined the walls of our former operation headquarters, but the tape was starting to lose its hold. The wires still ran to the East Wing, a reminder of the days when boys from the Blackthorne Institute had seemed like a mission—back when missions had been about getting us ready for the real world; before the real world cornered us on a rooftop in Massachusetts.

Liz must have followed my gaze and read my mind,

because I heard her say, "Have you heard from . . . you know . . . Zach?"

I thought back to the swirling images that had filled my mind before I'd blacked out, and almost asked, "Do hallucinations after a head injury count?" But I didn't because A) I may very well have been going crazy. And B) for a Gallagher Girl, "Boy crazy" might be the most dangerous kind of crazy there is.

So instead I turned to look out the window and watched the long line of limousines winding down Highway 10, carrying my classmates back to the safety of our walls.

It was the same scene I'd witnessed for years—the same cars, the same girls. But in the next instant the scene totally changed. Vans—dozens of them—sped down the highway, skidding into ditches on the side of the road. People bolted out and started adjusting satellite dishes and equipment. Helicopters swarmed around the school.

"Oh. My. Gosh," I mumbled, still staring, feeling Bex and Liz crowd around the window on either side of me. I looked at my best friends as sirens began screeching through the still, quiet air: "CODE RED CODE RED CODE RED."

"What does it mean?" Liz screamed. Bex and I just smiled.

"Macey's coming home."

Chapter Six

It doesn't take a genius to know that the whole world can change in an instant, and as soon as I hurried out of the secret passageway and into the second-floor corridor I could see and hear and feel the difference. For days the halls had felt like a tomb. But now, instead of stone silence, the whole school was on fire (without actually burning, of course).

Red lights flashed and blurred. To my right, a poster advertising the chance to spend a semester in Paris slid down over a display of secret writing techniques used through the ages (which wasn't entirely necessary since, this month, it was featuring invisible ink).

As we ran past the Encryption and Encoding department, I saw the plaque on the door flipping over to read Ivy League Liaison Office.

Our school was going undercover, pulling on its disguises as deftly as any seasoned operative can do, and as Bex, Liz, and I ran against a current of eighth graders on their way to stand guard outside the Protection and Enforcement barn, I couldn't help but smile. After all, it had been three hundred and sixty-four days since Macey had come to us during a Code Red. It seemed only fitting that she would come back to us in one.

But as we ran through the Hall of History, I watched Gillian Gallagher's sword disappear into the case that holds our deepest treasure, and something hit me: we wouldn't have a Code Red for Macey.

We were having a Code Red for Macey *and whoever was coming with her*.

The door to my mother's office eased open. Inside, I saw our headmistress, wearing her best suit and a grim expression. "I guess we're ready for our close-ups?" she was saying.

As soon as we stepped into the office I heard more voices.

"Now America waits for its first glimpse of Macey McHenry, the brave young woman who has so recently been thrust into the spotlight—and into danger."

(Evidently, one of the Code Red precautions for making the headmistress's office look like a regular school is to add a TV.)

Bex flipped through channel after channel until we came to the image that made us all freeze.

"And here we are," a tall correspondent said into a microphone as she strolled down a familiar stretch of Highway 10, "outside the gates of the Gallagher Academy for Exceptional Young Women, where one exceptional young woman will be returning shortly, after the most traumatic incident of her life. And the question remains: Will these walls be enough to keep Macey McHenry safe?"

The sirens finally stopped. My mother said, "It's time."

Okay, here's the thing you need to know about spy schools— it's not about hiding them. Nope. Because, let's face it, spy schools have students, and students have parents, and parents are going to ask questions. According to Liz, non-spy parents are really big on obvious questions like "so where exactly *is* your school?" (*Spy* parents are far more likely to hack into a government database or put a GPS unit in your tooth or something.) In any case, you kinda need an actual school to present to the world; but like everything else about my life, my school wasn't exactly what it seemed.

Following my mother down the sweeping Grand Stairs, I couldn't help but think that our first line of defense was about to be put to the test, because even though the Gallagher Academy has never exactly hidden (it is a big, honking mansion, after all), my school has never gone looking for the spotlight.

When Gillian Gallagher converted her family's home into a school where young women could learn the covert skills that no men would ever teach them, she'd had the good sense not to put "The Gallagher Academy—Educating Government Operatives Since 1865" on the sign. Instead she'd called it a finishing school for the most outstanding girls of the day. Our cover has evolved with the times, but our ultimate mission has stayed the same: make sure no one ever knows just how exceptional we really are. Which, let's face it, is a whole lot easier when there aren't two dozen national news crews videotaping your every move.

When we reached the foyer, I could have sworn that the entire student body was holding their breath as my mother pulled open the double doors and stepped outside.

Warm sunlight beamed down. My stomach growled, and for a second I wondered what our chef was making for the welcome-back dinner. But when I saw three big black SUVs pulling through the gate, I totally lost my appetite.

"Secret Service," my mother whispered to us as they started down the winding lane. I remembered that even Macey's protectors wouldn't know what we really do behind our walls.

An efficient-looking man with a touch of gray sprinkled through his dark hair climbed out of one of the vehicles and walked toward us. "Ms. Morgan? Agent Hughes. We spoke on the phone."

"Yes," Mom said. "You're the agent in charge of the McHenry family's security detail. That is the term, isn't it?" she asked, one hand against her chest as if this were totally new territory for her.

The man smiled and nodded. "Yes, ma'am," he told her. "Now, I don't want you to worry about anything. Our agents will be responsible for Ms. McHenry's security. They'll answer any questions you have and keep you informed of what the Service needs from you. No one is expecting you to think like a security professional."

"That is a relief," my mother told him in the most utterly believable, non-ironic voice I've ever heard.

(Have I mentioned lately that my mom is the BEST SPY EVER?!)

"Oh, I'm sorry," my mother said, looking from Agent Hughes and then to us. "Please allow me to introduce Macey's roommates. This is Elizabeth Sutton and Rebecca Baxter, and my daughter, Cammie."

But Agent Hughes wasn't listening. He was too busy staring at me—the girl who is hardly ever stared at.

"You were on the roof?" he asked, but it wasn't a question. He stepped closer; his gaze flashed across the bandage on my head, then his eyes searched mine. "Don't you worry about anything, young lady. We're going to take good care of all of you."

I nodded and looked away, thinking about my cover—I was supposed to be scared and tired and ready to let someone else fight for Macey.

Then I remembered that the best covers always have their roots in the truth.

"And the walls circle the entire grounds?" Agent Hughes asked as we walked around the campus.

"Yes," my mom said.

"According to the blueprints, you do have security cameras?" His gaze drifted along our ivy-covered walls.

"Yes," Mom said calmly. "Some."

(Actually, there are 2,546, but for obvious reasons she didn't share that.)

"Well," the agent went on, "I'm sure our people can consult with you on how to"—he seemed to be considering his words—"tighten things up a bit."

"Yes," my mom said with a glance toward me—her daughter, who had been slipping through the Gallagher Academy defenses for years. "That would be *most helpful.*"

And then panic set in. The Secret Service was going to be "tightening" things?

"As the advance team told you last week, we'll be placing one of our agents with Ms. McHenry."

The Secret Service was going to be "placing" people?

"Full-time," Agent Hughes added. "Someone to go with her to classes. Live here. Accompany her everywhere she goes."

The Secret Service was going to be "accompanying" us places?

I looked at Bex and Liz, watched them swallow the same terror I was feeling. Our school has prepared us for a lot of things, but I had to wonder if anything had prepared us for that.

But the surprises were only just beginning, because then my mother smiled and said, "Of course."

The agent walked ahead, appraising our grounds, our walls, our life. At the end of our long (and heavily protected) lane, satellite dishes rose from news trucks, ready to beam pictures of our school around the world, and I knew the most dangerous thing in our history was about to happen in front of this man's very eyes.

And there was nothing any of us could do to stop it.

"Oh," Agent Hughes said when the gates parted for one last car. "Right on schedule."

The limo turned onto the drive, but instead of pulling closer to the mansion, it stopped. Men in dark suits swarmed the car, and I remembered how, a year ago, a car just like that had brought Macey to us. Like déjà vu, Senator and Mrs. McHenry climbed from the backseat and stood framed between our great stone gates.

I could hear the reporters' chatter in the distance. The flashing bulbs of their cameras sparkled even in the summer sun.

And then the car door opened again.

And just like that the déjà vu was over.

A year before, Macey had stepped from the backseat of a nearly identical car, but this time, instead of combat boots, she wore pumps almost exactly like her mother's. Her short skirt and diamond nose stud were replaced with modest black pants, a sweater, and a sling.

At first I hoped her clothing was the only difference; but I barely recognized the girl who allowed her mother to hug her tightly, who didn't protest when her father took her good hand and lifted their united fists toward the sky.

Bex cut me a look that said *Are you sure you were the one with head trauma?* but I just watched the three McHenrys push past the cameras and the questions and start toward the school. Back to us. I thought about the girl who had come to us last fall and the one who had left last spring and, finally, about the young woman who had shivered by a lake, and I wondered which one of Macey's cover identities she was going to be now.

As they came closer I waited for her to catch my eye and smile that mischievous smile she'd given me outside her parents' suite in Boston, but when I stepped forward, a broad body in a dark suit moved to block my path.

"Excuse me, miss," the Secret Service agent said. It was the first time any of them had seen me as a threat, but I didn't take it as a compliment.

Behind me, I heard my mother say, "Senator, Mrs. McHenry, it's so nice to see you both again. I'm only sorry it has to be under such troubling circumstances." She gestured toward the front doors. "Won't you come in?"

Just when I felt myself getting pushed out of the picture, the procession stopped. The senior senator from Virginia stepped toward me and said, "Cammie?" He placed his large hands on both of my shoulders, gripping tightly.

"Thank you," he said, and I could have sworn I heard his voice crack. When he looked into my eyes, I couldn't help myself: I felt my lips tremble. My vision blurred. It was easy to remember what having a father feels like as the senator whispered, "And I'm so sorry."

It might have been about the sweetest, most genuine moment in McHenry family history, if Macey's mother hadn't then turned to her daughter and whispered, "Go to the bathroom and put some concealer on that." She pointed to the bruise at the corner of Macey's eye. "Really," she told her daughter, "there's no need to look like a common street thug when there aren't even any cameras around."

And, like that, the moment was over.

Chapter Seven

There are many things to love about the welcome-back dinner.

1. Hearing what everyone did over their summer vacation (which is probably far more interesting at a school where there's a very good possibility that the stories include actual gunfire).

2. The fact that even though Grandma Morgan probably makes the best chicken and dumplings in the entire world, our chef used to work at the White House, and sometimes a girl just needs a little crème brûlée.

3. Gossip.

But that night, neither 1 nor 2 could really hold a candle to 3. At all.

"So, Cammie," Tina Walters said as she squeezed onto

the bench across from me, squishing Liz and Anna Fetterman together, "I heard you put three of them in the hospital."

"Tina," I sighed, "it wasn't like that."

Eva Alvarez was trying to sign Macey's cast, which was difficult because the campaign manager didn't want anything to obscure the big Winters-McHenry sticker already plastered on Macey's forearm. Bex was picking apart one of the rolls from the basket on the table (even though the teachers hadn't made their entrance yet and, therefore, eating could be punishable by death—or at the very least some serious Culture and Assimilation extra homework if Madame Dabney caught you.)

"And, Macey"—Tina whirled on the girl beside me— "rumor has it *you* were spotted in a compromising position with a certain future first son."

And just like that, everything got quiet again.

The entire junior class turned and stared, but I kept doing exactly what I had been: studying Macey. The snob who had come to us a year before would have scoffed; the girl who had covered two years' worth of advanced encryption in nine months might have rolled her eyes; but the girl beside me simply said, "Someone needs better sources."

It was the first time she'd spoken, and something in her tone made me wonder whether or not the girl by the lake was gone for good.

"So, who thinks we'll have to stay in Code Red all semester?" Anna Fetterman asked, not even trying to disguise the fear in her voice.

My roommates and I all looked at each other, the scene that we'd witnessed outside playing over all of our faces.

"Well, they *are* going to give you a full-time Secret Service detail, aren't they?" Tina asked.

Macey nodded.

"Maybe the Secret Service . . . you know"—Liz hesitated and then lowered her voice to a whisper—"*knows.*"

But all I could think about were the agents who had questioned me after Boston, the lies I'd already had to tell to keep our secret safe.

"Mom wouldn't," I started. "She wouldn't agree to that."

"It would be a pretty good test, though, wouldn't it?" Bex asked. I could tell by the tone of her voice that she was already gearing up for the challenge—the thought of bringing the outside world inside our walls, the danger, the risk, the possibility of knocking a member of the United States Secret Service unconscious at some point during the semester.

"What if you get a guy agent?" Courtney Bauer joined in the conversation. "Aren't all the Secret Service guys really hot?"

"They're okay," Macey said nonchalantly, as if she'd seen hotter (and I'm pretty sure she had).

"What if he's like, *Mr. Solomon* hot?" Anna asked and then blushed.

As much as I wanted to join in and feel excited about a possible (hot) newcomer, all I could think was that there was too much risk and danger already. I remembered the feeling in my stomach as the elevator took us to the roof in Boston. I could have stopped it then. If I'd been focused, if my mind had been anywhere except on a certain boy, my school and my sisterhood might still be safe. But instead, a generation of geniuses were sitting around stealing dinner rolls and discussing the theoretical biceps of the person who might jeopardize our entire way of life (and whether or not he would actually take a bullet for Macey if the need arose).

Suddenly the doors at the back of the room swung open, and my mother appeared, leading our teachers down the center of the huge room.

I saw the new face of Mr. Smith, our Countries of the World instructor, who is one of the more paranoid government operatives on the planet and chooses to prove it by getting a new face every year during summer vacation. I heard the muttering of more than a hundred teenage girls as they realized that this year Mr. Smith's new face was . . . hot.

And then a hush went through the crowd, because our teachers were not alone.

Macey's parents were walking through the doors, waving and shaking hands, followed by a member of the United States Secret Service. I'm pretty sure if there had been any babies to kiss, The Senator would have done it.

There are a lot of scary things about being a Gallagher Girl, but having people who don't belong in your school walk inside it is high on the list. And I knew that we were being welcomed back to a very different school.

"Ooh," Liz said beside me. With wide eyes, she watched

Macey's parents greet our Culture and Assimilation professor, Madame Dabney.

Across the table, Bex grinned and whispered, "Pop quiz?"

"Welcome back, ladies," my mother said from the front of the room. "I can honestly say that I have never felt so glad to have you all here . . ." She paused; her gaze swept over the room, which instantly grew dim as the sun slipped below the horizon. If I hadn't known better, I might have sworn I heard my mother's voice crack as she finished, "safe and sound."

No one whispered. No one giggled or teased. What had happened to Macey (and to me) hadn't been some wild tale that we'd carried back from our summer vacations. It was real. And no one felt like laughing anymore.

"As you know, the eyes of the world are now upon the Gallagher Academy," Mom went on. I couldn't help glancing at the McHenrys to see if they guessed my mother's secret meaning, but the two of them kept nodding the same somber nods that must be second nature for anyone with their name on a ballot.

"We must learn and we must persevere. We must be careful and we must be brave. And most importantly"—right then it seemed as if a hundred girls sat up a little straighter, literally rising to the challenge—"we must protect our sisterhood." Her voice grew a little stronger. "And our sisters."

I don't know for sure how many active Gallagher Girls

there are in the world. Hundreds. Thousands. We disappear into society and do our jobs without a word of thanks or any hope of praise. I may be the Chameleon, but in truth, every Gallagher Girl has to be somewhat invisible. Yet now, we were all in the spotlight.

"There are things that are expected of us," my mom went on. "For that reason, there will be some changes this semester."

A slight murmur went through the crowd.

"*All* lessons will take place inside the safety of the primary mansion." Senator McHenry nodded as if this seemed like a good idea, not really understanding *how* good, considering that a paparazzo with a telephoto lens might have some questions if he ever caught a teenage girl practicing a perfect Forenstyl Flip on a three-hundred-pound member of the maintenance staff.

"Also, as far as our most notable student of the moment is concerned, we will be enforcing a strict *no comment* policy," Mom continued. "Be prepared, ladies. People are going to want to hear how Macey is coping." I glanced at the girl beside me, wondering the same thing. "But they're not going to hear it from us."

Gallagher Girls keep secrets—that's what we do. And that mission had never felt so personal.

"And perhaps the biggest change of all," Mom said slowly. I felt the room lean closer. "This semester we will be welcoming a member of the McHenry's security detail into this school for Macey's protection."

I can't swear to it or anything, but for a second her eyes locked on me. "The security of Macey McHenry will *not* change what and how we learn. To that end, let's welcome Agent Abigail Cameron, who will be responsible for Ms. McHenry's security detail."

The room around me filled with noise and movement, but in my mind, things were suddenly quiet and slow. A woman with long dark hair and gorgeous green eyes had appeared at the back of the room.

"As it so happens, Agent Cameron is a graduate of the Gallagher Academy and therefore *uniquely* qualified to give Macey the best protection possible."

I know, having aced my lipreading midterm the previous semester, that the hall was a chorus of "Wow, she's pretty"s and "Wait, who's that?"s.

I know that every Gallagher Girl in the Grand Hall was looking at the woman walking through the room, thinking, *This is our sister.* But not me. All I could do was stare at her and whisper, "Aunt Abby?"

Chapter eight

When you've spent four years living with a certain British secret agent-in-training who loves to practice spontaneous attacks and self-defense maneuvers when you're brushing your teeth, it takes a lot to knock you off guard. So I like to consider myself the kind of person who can keep a straight face during just about anything. Or . . . well . . . almost anything.

I tried to remember the last time I'd seen my mother's sister—not since before Mom left the CIA, not since before I started school here. Not since before . . . Dad. And yet there she was, twenty feet away and walking closer.

Her hair was longer than I remembered, past her shoulders now. She was still thin and athletic, but she seemed shorter somehow, and then, genius that I am, I realized that maybe I was just taller.

"Hey, Cam," Bex whispered, jabbing me in the ribs, "isn't Cameron your mom's maiden name?"

"Yeah," I murmured as if it were just a big coincidence.

I studied her every move as she wove between the tables; she was the embodiment of what every girl in the room wanted to be when she grew up.

"She seems sort of . . . familiar," Liz said, and I could almost hear her mind working, gears turning, as if my aunt's face were a code she was trying to crack.

Then Abby winked at me, and, for Bex, the pieces fell into place. "No way!" She was pointing between my aunt and my mother as if memorizing every detail of their unmistakable family resemblance. "That's your aunt—"

"Shhh!" I whispered, cutting her off. After all, Tina Walters was only a few feet away; the McHenrys and Agent Hughes were at the front of the room; there were at least a dozen reasons why this was not the best time to go through the entire Cameron family tree, not the least of which was that I was already way more notorious around there than any chameleon should rightfully be.

My mother was the headmistresss.

I'd had an illegal (sort of) relationship with a normal boy who had crashed (literally) my Covert Operations midterm last December.

And the last time several members of the student body had seen me, I'd been kissing a boy from the rival spy school in the middle of the foyer during finals week!

I was *not* invisible anymore. And something told me that having my aunt leading Macey's security detail wasn't going to help matters. At all. Because even though I hadn't seen her in years, I was sure that if there's one thing Abby is not, it's invisible.

"Cam." Liz's voice was soft. "You look like you've seen a ghost."

Aunt Abby finally made it to the front of the room, and I just sat there feeling like maybe . . . I had.

———

QUESTIONS I NEVER WANTED TO HEAR AGAIN AFTER THAT NIGHT

1. Did Zach call/write/break into and/or bug my grandparents' house over summer vacation? (Because the answer was no.)

2. Did I know that the news channels only showed part of the footage from the attack in Boston, but it happened to be the part where my skirt blew up? Way up! (Because, sadly, the answer was something I couldn't forget.)

3. Did I think Mr. Smith's new face made him look kind of . . . hot? (Because *Smith* and *hot* were two words I never wanted to hear together.)

4. Where had Aunt Abby worked? (Because I didn't know.)

5. What had Aunt Abby done? (Because I couldn't even guess.)

6. Why would an operative in the prime of her career come out of the field to take over Macey's security detail when there had to be a lot more senior operatives who would have dropped everything to keep one of their own safe? (Because I didn't want to think about it.)

––––––––

"Come on, Cam," Liz pleaded the next morning, the lack of significant intel finally weighing on her. "She's your *aunt*. You've got to know something."

I just shrugged. "Liz, she's a deep-cover covert operative—you know how it is."

Liz stared at me blankly, but Bex nodded. After all, her parents were with MI6, so she *did* know. Better than anyone.

"Do you think she'll be teaching a class?" Liz gripped her extra-credit project for Mr. Mosckowitz as if her life depended on it (because, when you're Liz, your life kinda does). "I tried hacking into Langley, and everything about her was classified. I mean, *seriously* classi—Ow!" Liz cried.

I'm not sure how she did it, but Elizabeth Sutton, the smartest Gallagher Girl in perhaps the history of Gallagher Girls, had just managed to cut her chin with a paper clip.

Bex laughed. Liz bled (but only a little). My stomach growled, and I felt the clock inside of me ticking again, telling me that it was time, so I grabbed my bag and called, "Come on. We don't want to be late."

I was already in the hall before I noticed someone was missing.

"Macey!" I yelled, pushing open the bathroom door. "We're heading down to—" But I couldn't finish. Because Macey McHenry, the girl with the physical appearance so perfect a supermodel might feel inferior, was changing her clothes *in the bathroom*. And then I saw why.

A bruise covered her entire side, green tinges bleeding into purple. Her elbow was still swollen to twice its normal size. I didn't have to hear her wince to know how much it hurt, and yet the look on her face said that having me witness her vulnerability was the most painful thing of all. Macey's pride was the one thing that had come away unscathed, and she was going to protect it if it killed her.

"Cam!" Bex yelled from outside. "We're hungry!"

"Go on," I called, my eyes still locked with Macey's in the mirror. "Macey's not letting me go without eyeliner." It must have been a believable cover story, because the door closed. The suite grew quiet, and Macey turned around.

Wordlessly, she held her arm out to me, and I eased her shirtsleeve over her cast. She turned back to the mirror but no longer met my eyes as she said, "Nobody finds out."

Bex would have thought it was cool. Liz would have calculated the exact amount of force it would have taken to do that kind of damage. Bruises like that usually earn you a week's worth of extra credit in P&E. But Macey didn't want to hear those things.

And it was just as well, because I didn't want to say them.

So I helped her into her school sweater wondering:

7. Did I think Macey was okay? (Because I was the only one who seemed to be asking it.)

Sometime in the night our school had reversed itself. The Code Red was over. The Senator and his entourage were gone. Bookshelves and paintings had spun around again, and in the Hall of History, Gilly's sword was gleaming in its protective case.

Everything seemed right. Everything seemed normal. Then I heard a voice I hadn't heard in a very long time say, "Hey, squirt."

My mom calls me kiddo. My friends call me Cam. Zach called me Gallagher Girl. But no nickname in history has ever had the same effect on me as "Squirt." I suddenly had the urge to spin around really, really fast and eat cotton candy until I was sick. But instead I just said, "Hi."

"Someone grew up."

"I'm sixteen," I said, which was about the dumbest thing ever, but I couldn't help it. Even geniuses have the right to be dumb sometimes. I felt Bex and Liz come from the Grand Hall to stand beside me. "Everyone, this is"—I gazed up at her, wondering how she could look almost exactly the same when almost everything in my life was different—"Aunt Abby?" It came out like a question, but it wasn't.

"Don't tell me," my aunt said as she turned to Bex, "*you* must be a Baxter."

Bex beamed. It didn't matter that the two of them had never met before. My aunt didn't wait on introductions. Which was just as well—Bex never waited on anything. "So how's your dad?"

"He's great," Bex said with a grin.

Abby winked. "Do me a favor and tell him Dubai at Christmas is no fun without him."

Beside me, I could practically feel Bex's mind spinning out of control, wondering about Dubai in December. But Abby didn't offer details; instead she just turned to Liz.

"Oooh," Abby said as she examined the fresh cut on her chin. "Paper clip?" she asked.

Liz's eyes got even wider. "How did you know that?"

Abby shrugged. "I've seen things."

I thought back to Mr. Solomon's cabin. Whenever he and my mother spoke about the things they'd seen and done, I wanted to hide from the details of their lives. But as Abby spoke, we hung on every word.

"Does Fibs still have that stash of the SkinAgain prototype in the lab?" my aunt asked.

"Isn't that a little"—Liz started—"strong?" (Which might have been a bit of an understatement, since I know for a fact the Gallagher Academy developed SkinAgain after an eighth grader fell into a vat of liquid nitrogen.)

Abby shrugged. "Not if you mix it with a little aloe. Rub some of that on, and no way that leaves a scar."

"Seriously?" Bex and Liz asked at the exact same time.

Abby leaned into the light. "Does this look like the face of a woman who survived a knife fight in Buenos Aires?"

Every girl in the foyer (by then there were quite a few) craned to look at her flawless, porcelain skin.

"That's not a good idea, Ms. McHenry," my aunt said, startling her admirers. I turned and saw Macey reaching for the front doors, and realized Abby had sensed her without even turning around. And just that quickly her skin stopped being the most amazing thing about her.

"I don't do breakfast," Macey said. (Which was a lie, but I didn't say so.) "I'm going for a walk."

At the sound of the word "breakfast," the girls in the foyer seemed to remember that they'd spent an entire summer without access to our chef's Belgian waffles. They filtered out, one by one, until it was just me, my three best friends in the world, and the woman who had taught me how to use a jump rope to temporarily paralyze a man when I was seven.

She stepped closer to Macey. "The security division noted two helicopters in the vicinity this morning—probably paparazzi looking for pictures of you—but until we're sure . . ." She eased between her protectee and the door. "You can't go outside. I'm sorry." She added that last part later, like an afterthought.

"Isn't that why *you're* here?" Macey reminded her and stepped toward the door again, but Abby casually cut her off.

"Actually, that's why I'm *here*." Abby pointed to her feet and leaned against the door. It might have been a casual gesture from another person, in another place. But as I looked from my aunt to Macey, I realized they were both strong. Both smart. Both used to being the prettiest girl in the room. The last time I'd had a feeling like that, it had involved Dr. Fibs's lab and two chemicals that are both potent, and volatile, and don't really like being put together under pressure.

"Rule number one, ladies," my aunt said. "Get careless . . . get caught."

As she walked away, Bex grabbed my arm and mouthed, "She's bloody awesome!"

Then, without turning around, Abby called, "I bloody know."

The rest of the morning was something of a blur.

Macey was in the junior level Countries of the World class, so she sat right beside me as Mr. Smith talked for forty-five minutes about the pros and cons of getting your cosmetic surgery at CIA-approved facilities. (Evidently, the work is very high quality, but since they don't technically "exist," the insurance paperwork is a nightmare!)

Madame Dabney gave a nice, relaxing refresher course on the basics: i.e. identifying every piece in a twenty-piece place setting (and the corresponding best methods in which each utensil could be used as a weapon).

Things seemed perfectly normal as we started down the

Grand Staircase and Liz headed toward Dr. Fibs's lab in the basement.

"See ya!" she called, which was okay. I'd gotten used to the idea that Liz was destined for the research-and-operations track while Bex and I were training for a life in the field.

It wasn't until I heard Macey say, "See you at lunch," that I remembered she was still behind the rest of us, academically.

As she set off for the freshman-level encryption course taught by Mr. Mosckowitz, Bex and I moved into the small passage beneath the Grand Staircase and stepped before a gilt-framed mirror. A thin laser beam scanned our faces, reading our retinal images. The eyes of the painting behind us flashed green, and a mirror slid aside, revealing the elevator to the most secret classrooms of the most secret school in the country.

But I didn't feel a rush. I wasn't thinking about pop quizzes or how Mr. Solomon looked that one time when we were doing wilderness reconnaissance exercises and he rolled up his sleeves.

Instead I just said, "Bex," and waited for my best friend's "Yeah."

"I'm worried about Macey."

"Why?" Bex asked, pressing her palm against the glass on the inside of the elevator. "She seems fine to me."

I placed my palm beside my best friend's. "That's what worries me."

Bex is black and I'm white. She's beautiful and I'm plain. She grew up in London and I spend my summers on a ranch in the middle of nowhere. She was born for fight and I was born for flight. But the way she looked at me reminded me that Bex and I are alike in all the ways that matter.

"I know something that'll make you feel better," she said.

"What?" I asked as the elevator around us rumbled to a start. My palm burned hot and I jerked my hand from the glass. An odd light unlike anything I'd ever seen before filled the car around us, and through an eerie purple glow, my best friend smiled.

"We're about to see Sublevel Two."

Chapter nine

When you're the first Gallagher Girl since Gilly herself to find and use the passageway behind the third-floor corridor that contained a million dollars worth of confederate coins, you might start thinking that the Gallagher mansion can't possibly surprise you anymore.

But you'd be wrong.

The car stopped. I knew the doors were about to slide open and reveal the most covert place we had ever seen. I held my breath, waiting. Then suddenly the car jerked backward, throwing us against the doors.

"Cam," Bex said as we hurtled at least a hundred feet further underground. "Is this supposed to be—" she started, but suddenly we were plunging downward again.

We halted. "PRESENT DNA, PLEASE," a mechanical voice rang through the car. A narrow slot appeared in the stainless-steel shell. It was exactly finger-size, so I reached out to touch it.

"Ouch!" I cried. A small pin had pricked me. Then it disappeared, and a fresh needle replaced it. A small drop of blood bubbled at the top of my finger.

"No way," Bex said, shaking her head emphatically. (And that's how I learned that the girl who once bragged she'd taken on an arms dealer in a sword fight in Cairo one spring break was actually afraid of needles.)

"PRESENT DNA, PLEASE," the voice demanded again, this time sounding slightly less patient, so Bex put her finger in just as the car stopped.

The doors slid open . . . and I knew that nothing about Sublevel One had prepared me for Sublevel Two.

It had been almost exactly a year since Bex and I had first laid eyes on Sublevel One. There the walls were made of stainless steel and frosted glass. Our footsteps had echoed. I'd always brought a sweater. Everything about it was cool and modern, like stepping inside the future—our future. But stepping inside Sublevel Two was . . . not.

Around me, other elevator doors were sliding open; other girls with bleeding fingers were stepping onto creaking, wide-planked oak floors.

The ceiling was a jigsaw puzzle of thick stone and heavy beams, and as I reached out to touch the rock walls, I realized there were no seams. No mortar. Just an indeterminable amount of limestone and earth separating us from the outside world.

My classmates stirred and turned, too busy taking in the

dimly lit space to notice the man who stepped out of the shadows and said, "Welcome to Sublevel Two." He turned and started down the gently sloping floors, leading us in a steady spiral. "I'd highly recommend paying attention, ladies," Mr. Solomon instructed. "First day is the last day you get a guide."

Corridors branched away from the spiraling walkway in a maze of stone. We passed arching doorways, and the incline grew steeper. One wide corridor was labeled, simply, STORAGE, but the doors that lined the hall were marked with everything from F, FALSE FLAG OPERATIONS; H, HITLER, ATTEMPTED ASSASSINATIONS OF. I'd always heard about secrets being locked in stone, but I'd never seen it with my own eyes until then.

We walked for what felt like five minutes. The air around us was damp and cool, and yet something told me that even in the dead of winter or heat of summer the temperature would never vary more than three degrees.

And then finally Joe Solomon came to a stop. As we stepped onto a floor of solid stone, I looked back up the spiraling walkway—at the corridors that branched like a maze—and suddenly I pitied the enemy agent who was ever foolish enough to try to penetrate this store of covert knowledge. And finally I smiled, wondering what on earth (or beneath it) could possibly lay in store on Sublevel Three.

"Covert operations." Mr. Solomon walked through a set of large double doors into a room twice as large as the library in the mansion above us. As in the library, a second-story walkway circled the room, and old-fashioned wooden tables were arranged in a U-like shape across the floor.

"The clandestine service . . ." our teacher talked on as the entire junior CoveOps class rushed to claim seats. "It's a life of being where you're not supposed to be—of doing what you're not supposed to do." There was a wooden chair at the front of the room, but instead of sitting, he gripped the back of it with both hands. It was the first thing about Covert Operations that felt familiar. "It means getting in, ladies." He searched the room. "And most important, it means getting out."

I thought about hotels and laundry chutes, and for a second my head hurt. I felt a little dizzy as our teacher said, "Exfiltrations are defined by two factors, Ms. Baxter. Name them."

"They take place in hostile territory," Bex said.

"Correct," Mr. Solomon replied, taking a step. He wrote Bex's response on an ancient rolling chalkboard at the front of the room. "That's one qualifier of an exfiltration. Ms. Fetterman, what's two?"

As we waited for Anna's response, I heard the chalk against the board. Everything was louder here, especially the clear bright voice that said, "No one ever knows about it."

Every head turned. I've never seen anyone command a room more effortlessly than Aunt Abby did when she said, "You rang, Joe?"

Oh. My. Gosh.

Maybe it was the spy in me . . . or the girl in me . . . or

the *niece* in me . . . but when Aunt Abby placed her hand on her hip, I could have sworn she was doing something that I hadn't thought any Gallagher Girl would ever dare to do: flirt with Joe Solomon!

"Agent Cameron," Mr. Solomon said. "So glad you could join us. The junior class . . ." He gestured toward us. Aunt Abby waved two fingers.

"Hi, girls."

". . . and I were just getting ready to discuss exfiltration operations." He dropped the chalk into the tray and slapped his hands together twice. "Thought you might lend a unique perspective to that topic."

"Oh, Mr. Solomon," Abby said with a smile, "you do know how to show a girl a good time."

She walked around the U of desks, scanning the walls, the cases of books, everything about Sublevel Two; and I realized that while I was seeing it for the first time, my aunt was seeing it *again* after a long time. I wondered if it might look different in the light of everything she'd learned since leaving.

"As I was saying," Mr. Solomon went on, "exfiltrations are critical. And they're hard—"

"Especially in Istanbul," Aunt Abby added softly, and our teacher laughed. It sounded like an inside joke, except spies don't make inside jokes! There's too much information "inside," and so that's where we keep it. But the craziest thing wasn't that Aunt Abby had made a joke. . . . It wasn't even that she was flirting. The craziest thing was that I was pretty sure that smiling and laughing were Mr. Solomon's way of flirting back!

There we were, in a cavern of stone and secrets, and yet it felt like my aunt had brought the sun in with her, illuminating a side of my teacher that I had never seen.

For the first time in weeks, my head didn't hurt. Boston was just a city in Massachusetts.

I might have been content to sit like that all day—all week. All year. But then the lights went out. At the back of the room an old-fashioned projector came to life, and an image was slicing through the dark.

"I'm sure you've all seen this before," Mr. Solomon said.

But I hadn't seen it. A chill ran through me as I realized . . . I'd lived it.

The entire class seemed to hold its breath while the film cut between different angles, different cameras, different news crews. Parts of the footage had been shown in an almost continual loop on every TV in the country for days, but as with most things we Gallagher Girls do, there was a lot more to the story, and that day we were seeing the uncensored version.

"What I'm about to show you is a nearly textbook example of a daylight exfiltration operation in an occupied area." I thought Mr. Solomon would look at me. I expected my aunt to ask if I was okay. I wanted someone to acknowledge that it wasn't a lesson—it was the hardest day of my life. But the only change in our teacher's voice was a sudden pause before he added, "Lucky for us, it didn't work."

And then I knew that we weren't there to study what Macey and I had done right. *We* weren't the seasoned professional operatives on the roof that day. We were just two girls who got lucky, and luck's not a skill that anyone can learn.

Dust kept dancing in the projector's light. At no point did anyone say, "If this is too much for you, Cammie, you can leave" or "Ms. Morgan, what were you thinking there?"

I was just another girl in the room, not the girl on the roof. The sounds were different there—just the buzz of my instructor's voice. The answering of questions. The muffled shouts of the camera operators as they jockeyed for position.

But in my head I saw the whirl of circling blades. I heard the grunts and kicks, the distant roar of the wind coming in off the harbor. In my mind, the film was clearer and slower as Preston fell to safety. And then I watched a masked figure ignore the son of a potential president, point to my best friend, and say the two words I hadn't truly heard before.

The room was dark.

The walls around us were thick.

And I'm pretty sure my aunt was the only person who heard me whisper, "Get *her*."

Chapter ten

There are things spies often carry with them: pocket litter, fake IDs, the occasional weapon-slash-camera-slash-hair accessory. But the heaviest things, I think, are the secrets. They can drown you if they let them. As I sat inside Sublevel Two that day, I knew the one I held was so heavy I might never see the surface again.

When class was over, the lights came on, and I listened as half of my classmates scattered to explore their new surroundings. I watched Mick Morrison corner Mr. Solomon with a dozen questions about the Marciano Theory and its proper use in urban settings, but the rest of the class stood huddled around Aunt Abby, who was doing a very dramatic reenactment of the time she'd had to sneak a nuclear engineer out of Taiwan during the rainy season.

"So then I told him, I know it's a rickshaw, but that doesn't mean it doesn't float!" Abby said.

Tina and Eva burst out laughing, but I knew Aunt Abby

was watching out of the corner of her eyes as I left the classroom and started up the long spiraling ramp that led to the mansion above us. I knew she was listening as Bex fell into step beside me and said, "Cam, slow down," as if it were possible for me to outpace her. (Which it isn't.)

But I just kept spiraling upward, remembering the words I had listened to but hadn't *heard*; recalling the attackers' indifference when Preston fell to safety over the side of the roof—the things I had watched but hadn't *seen*.

"I was an idiot!" I snapped.

"You were brilliant," Bex said, and from any other girl in any other school those words might have sounded like lip service. But not this girl. Not this school. From Bex, it was an undisputed fact, and she was willing to take on anyone who said otherwise.

"Two girls in this school could have done what you did," She cocked an eyebrow. "And you're the other one."

As we reached the elevators and stepped inside, I thought about how there are two types of secrets: the kind you *want* to keep in, and the kind you don't *dare* to let out.

I could have looked at Bex. I could have lowered my voice, and there, in that tiny elevator a hundred feet beneath the ground, I could have been certain that no one could possibly overhear.

But my mother and Mr. Solomon were the two best spies I know, and they hadn't told Macey. They hadn't told *me*.

As the elevator doors slid open, I heard the sound of

girls coming down the stairs above us. The smell of lunch drifted from the Grand Hall. Things move through our mansion as fast as fire sometimes. And that's when I knew I had the second type of secret.

I didn't dare to set it free.

Instead I carried it into the Grand Hall and sat down at the juniors' table for lunch, barely looking up until I heard Eva Alvarez announce, "Mail's here."

She dropped a postcard on the table in front of me, and immediately I recognized the ruby slippers from the National Museum of American History and *The Wizard of Oz* and, most important, from the very place where Zach and I had first seen each other for what we really were.

This isn't a hallucination, I told myself. This is real, I thought as I turned it over and studied the handwriting that, last spring, I'd watched wash away in the rain.

And I read the words "Be careful."

I spent the rest of that week trying to talk to Aunt Abby alone, but the problem was, from that point on, my aunt was *never* alone.

"Um, Aunt Abby, can we . . . talk?" I asked Monday night after supper, but Abby just smiled and started for the door. Unfortunately, half the sophomore class started with her.

"Sure, squirt. I was just going to go to teach these guys this really cool move with a garden hose. Wanna come?"

When I saw her in the foyer Tuesday afternoon, I asked,

"Hey, Aunt Abby, do you maybe have some time to . . . catch up . . . tonight?"

"Ooh, sorry, Camster," she told me as she started walking Macey to P&E. "Fibs has asked me to help him whip up a batch of this superpowerful coma-inducing cream I learned how to make in the Amazon. It could take all night."

Everywhere I turned I heard questions like, "Hey, Cammie, has Abby ever shown you that thing she did in Portugal with a bobby pin?"

Or "Well, I heard that five more senior operatives were begging to take Macey's detail, but the deputy director of the CIA *himself* called and asked Abby to take the job."

By Saturday, it was starting to feel like the one story Aunt Abby wouldn't tell was the only one I wanted to hear.

And, by Sunday, it had started to rain.

The halls seemed dimmer than usual for that early in the semester as I walked through the empty corridors on my way to my mother's office. When I passed the window seat on the second floor, I couldn't resist pulling back the red velvet curtains and peering through the wavy glass.

Heavy gray clouds hung low in the sky, but the trees were lush and green in the forest. Our walls were still tall and strong, and beyond them, not a single news van sat. I thought for a second that maybe the worst of it was over, but then a flash of lightning slashed through the sky, and I knew the storm was just beginning.

"Cammie!" Mom's voice called through the Hall of History, and I turned away from the glass.

Walking toward my mother's office, I couldn't help notice that she was smiling as if this were exactly how the first Sunday night after summer vacation was supposed to be—except this time it was definitely different. Because first, there was music. Loud music. Fast music. Music that was definitely *not* of the Culture and Assimilation variety!

And second, the food didn't smell terrible. Sure, it didn't smell as good as the aromas drifting from the Grand Hall, but it didn't look like the smoke (and/or hazardous materials) detectors had gone off yet, and that was a very good sign.

But as soon as I reached the door to my mother's office, I could see that what really set this Sunday night apart was that, this time, my mother was not alone.

"Hey, squirt. I'm crashing." My aunt winked as she pulled a grape from a bowl of fruit on the corner of my mother's desk. "Your mom and cooking," Abby said, grabbing me by the hand and spinning me around to the music, "*this*, I had to see."

"No one is forcing you to eat anything," Mom chided, but Abby just kept dancing, pulling me in and out until she whispered in my ear, "I've got an antidote for ninety-nine percent of the food-borne illnesses known to man in my purse, just in case."

And then I couldn't help myself. I laughed. For a second, it seemed right. For a second, it seemed safe. Everything was different . . . but familiar. The dancing. The music. The sounds and smells of Mom making her famous (in a bad way) goulash. It was as if I were having flashes of someone else's life. And then it hit me: it was *my* life. With Dad.

Dad used to listen to that music. Dad and I used to dance in our kitchen in D.C.

And suddenly I didn't feel like dancing anymore.

Mom watched me walk to the radio and turn down the volume.

"Oh, Cam," my aunt said with a sigh. "Look at you. All grown up and breaking hearts . . ." She raised her eyebrows. "And rules. Honestly, as an aunt, I don't know which makes me prouder."

"Abigail," Mom warned softly.

"Rachel," my aunt mimicked her sister's motherly tone.

"Perhaps the United States Secret Service should not be encouraging rule-breaking—especially at this particular school during this particular year."

"Perhaps the headmistress of the Gallagher Academy should try to remember that a spy's life is, by definition, rules-optional," my aunt lectured back.

"And while we're on the subject," Mom said, her voice rising, "perhaps the United States Secret Service should consider that it might be unwise to tell Madame Dabney's eighth graders how to make their own chloroform out of Kleenex and lemon wedges?"

"Yeah, I couldn't believe they hadn't figured out how to do that yet," Abby said, as if the standards for her sisterhood had gone down considerably.

"That technique was banned in 1982!"

"Hey, Joe said—"

"I don't care what Joe says!" Mom snapped, and this time her voice carried fire. "Abigail, rules exist for a reason. Rules exist because when people don't follow them, *people get hurt.*" The words lingered in the air. My mom seemed to be shaking as she finished. "Or maybe you've forgotten."

I've known Aunt Abby my whole life, but I've never seen her look like she looked then. She seemed torn between tears and fury while the storm raged outside and the goulash congealed and I wondered whether any of us would ever feel like dancing again.

"Rachel, I—"

"Get *her.*"

I don't know why I said it. One minute I was standing there watching them argue, and the next, the secret I'd carried with me all the way from Sublevel Two was breaking free.

Mom inched closer. Abby stepped away. And outside, the rain was falling against the mansion walls like the tide.

"What did you say, Cammie?" my mother asked in the manner of someone who already knows the answer to her question.

"I remembered . . ." I sank to the leather sofa. Mom inched closer, but behind her, Aunt Abby gave an almost imperceptible shake of her head—a warning. Be careful what you wish for. "I remembered something . . . about Boston. I put Preston on that window-washing thing, and they didn't really . . . care." Mom was easing onto the coffee table in front of me, moving slowly as if afraid to wake me from that terrible dream. "They said get *her*."

"Cam—" Mom started, but flashes filled my eyes again—a gray door, a black helicopter, and finally a white piece of paper fluttering to the ground.

"Preston's agenda," I whispered, but this time I didn't look at my mother—I looked at my aunt. "He was never supposed to be there, was he?"

Mom started to say something, but Aunt Abby walked past her and dropped onto the leather couch beside me. "Nope."

Some people might wonder why it mattered—we'd known for weeks that Macey was in danger. But sitting there, listening to the storm that had been a long time coming, I couldn't help but feel like it made all the difference in the world. The kidnappers weren't there for the son and daughter of two of the most powerful families in the country—they were there for only one of them.

And she was one of my best friends.

"It's true, kiddo," Mom said. "Preston Winters wasn't supposed to be there, so we can only assume that he wasn't the target."

I nodded. She smoothed my hair. But nothing could keep my heart from pounding as I asked, "Who were they?"

"More than three hundred groups have claimed credit for the attack," my aunt said, then added with a shrug, "which means at least 299 of them are lying."

"The ring," I said, closing my eyes and seeing the image that was burned into my mind. "I drew you a picture of that ring. Have you—"

"We're looking into it, kiddo," Mom said softly. I bit my lip, needing to know where at least some of the pain I was feeling was coming from.

"Why Macey?" I blurted, turning to my mother.

"She's the daughter of very powerful people, Cam. They have very powerful enemies."

And then I asked the question more terrifying than anything I'd seen on the roof. "Is she going to be okay?"

My mother and aunt looked at each other, two CoveOps veterans who had seen enough to know that there was no easy answer to my question. "The Secret Service is good, Cam," my mother said. "Your aunt Abby is very good." She looked at my aunt as if no amount of sibling rivalry could ever come between them. So I sat there for a long time thinking about sisters. About our sisterhood.

And then suddenly it seemed funny. It seemed crazy. We were in the middle of the Gallagher Academy, where the people are both crazy and really, really good at being crazy about security. Of course Macey was going to be okay.

"Well, at least we already go to the safest school in the world. And it's not like Macey's going anywhere, right?" I said with a smile—totally not expecting my aunt to smile back and say, "Yeah . . . well . . . Cam, have you ever been to Cleveland?"

Chapter ELEVEN

Ohio has twenty electoral votes and a history of high voter turnout. It has a governor from one party and two senators from the other. In September, it also had a lot of women who were unsure about who to vote for but who were certain about one thing: Macey McHenry was a brave, brave girl for surviving what happened to her in Boston.

Macey McHenry was going to be worth a lot of votes.

And so she was going there. Alone.

Well . . . if by alone you mean with one of the most honored Gallagher Girls in years (who, reportedly, looks a little like me when I wear my hair back), a caravan of fourteen Secret Service agents of her own personal detail, and at least thirty advance team members who were tracking her father's every move. But in the most important sense she was alone. Because she was going without us.

Monday morning, Macey was up at five a.m. and together we all walked her downstairs, where the smell of cinnamon rolls wafted in from the kitchen. Outside, the sun was coming up in the distance. A hazy light fell over the horizon, and through the windows I could see the guards doing a sweep of the woods.

Liz was wearing her $E=Mc^2$ pajamas, and Bex's hair was looking particularly out of control, but still we paraded Macey through the mansion until we saw Aunt Abby.

She wore a dark gray pantsuit with a plain white blouse. A little plastic earpiece was already pinned to her collar, the wires disappearing down the inside of her jacket. She looked the part—she *was* the part. And then we handed Macey off to her without a word, the changing of the guard.

And then I went and took a shower.

And then I ate a cinnamon roll.

And I didn't hear a thing Mr. Smith said about ancient Rome and the catacombs, which if you know where to look, still provide pretty awesome access to the city.

All day long, it seemed like people kept saying exactly what I was thinking.

"Well, I guess she's probably there by now," Tina said after breakfast.

"Macey is going to get to see so many cool protection tactics," Eva remarked on our way to COW.

"She's with Abby," Liz said on our way down the Grand Staircase.

"And Abby rocks," Bex reminded me just as we parted ways with Liz and headed to the elevator for Sublevel Two.

From a purely intellectual standpoint I knew Macey was

as well protected as she could possibly be, but Mr. Solomon had been teaching us for a year that being a spy isn't always about intellect—it's about instincts. And right then my instincts were telling me that it was going to be a very long day.

And that was *before* Mr. Solomon met us at the entrance to Sublevel Two with a stack of Winters-McHenry T-shirts and said, "Let's go."

I'd been in a helicopter with Mr. Solomon twice before. The first time I'd been blindfolded. The second, I'd just found out that there was *another* top secret spy school . . . *for boys*! But that day, boys and blindfolds seemed easy in comparison.

"Security threats come in how many forms, Ms. Alvarez?" Mr. Solomon asked.

"Five," Eva said, even though, technically, we hadn't covered that chapter yet.

"And who can tell me what they are?" our teacher went on.

"Long range, short range, suicide, static . . ." Bex rattled, not to show off, but more like she had to say them—like they'd been on her mind for too long and she had to set them free.

"That's four," Mr. Solomon told us.

The blades of the chopper were spinning; the ground beneath us was roaring by—trees and hills, rivers and highways, towns full of normal schools and normal kids and people who would never ever know the answer to our teacher's questions.

"Internal," I said so softly that with the spinning blades and gushing winds I wondered for a second if anyone heard.

But we're Gallagher Girls. We hear everything.

"That's right," Mr. Solomon told us. "And that's the big one."

I told myself that he wasn't talking about Macey—that he didn't mean that what had happened in Boston had been orchestrated by someone *inside*, someone close. But rather he was speaking in general terms, reminding us all of what we knew too well, that traitors are the most dangerous people of all.

"You're going to see a lot of things today, ladies. Seasoned operatives working in the field with one primary objective. It's not about intel, and it's not about ops. It's about protection today, pure and simple."

In my mind I was already running through the scenarios that only a man like Joe Solomon could come up with. I was imagining what tests could possibly be waiting on the ground.

Bex must have been thinking along those same lines, because she asked, "What's our mission?"

"It's a hard one," Mr. Solomon warned, then smiled. "Just watch. Just listen. Just learn."

Gallagher Girls are asked to do hard things. All the time. But until that day I never really knew that the hardest mission of all is to do nothing.

After all, it's one thing to take a group of highly

trained teenage future spies and drop them off in a crowd of thousands and tell them to find the potential security threat. It's quite another to take those same girls, equip them with comms units tuned to the same frequency as the Secret Service (not that the Secret Service actually *knew* or anything), and tell them to sit back and enjoy the show.

I don't even like letting someone else put the syrup on my waffles (I have a system), so letting other people be in charge of Macey's safety . . . well . . . let's just say it was a little out of my comfort zone.

And if that wasn't bad enough, the jeans that someone had packed for me to change into were a little on the snug side. And I don't know about everyone else, but Bex Baxter is the only girl I know who can enter and exit a helicopter without having it do really unfortunate things to her hair.

Most of all, I wanted to pretend that I still believed I lived in a world where hair and jeans really mattered. But I didn't. So I just thought about my mission and stared out into the crowd.

And then I disappeared.

———

THE ESSENTIALS OF BEING A CHAMELEON
By Cameron Ann Morgan

1. It's very important, at all times, to look like you belong.

2. When #1 is difficult, try pointing to imaginary people and walking purposefully toward no one.

3. Stillness. Stillness is key (except when you're doing #2) because people see motion more easily than they see things. So when in doubt, freeze.

4. It totally helps if you aren't all that special looking (in either really good or really bad ways).

5. Acquaint yourself with your surroundings ASAP.

6. Dress in a way that isn't flashy, fashionable, ugly, or obscene.

7. Hiding is for amateurs.

"This is . . . wow," Bex said ten minutes after we'd arrived at the park . . . or what I think was supposed to be a park.

A long grassy promenade covered at least two city blocks. Beautiful historic buildings lined the space, but at the far end, someone had erected a stage. Bleachers circled behind it, facing the lawn, and from where Bex and I stood it seemed like half of Ohio had come out to see Macey's triumphant return.

Over the loudspeakers I heard a local politician trying to make the people on the bleachers behind him chant

"Winters" while the people on the grass in front of the stage were told to yell "McHenry."

"Are American politics always so . . . crazy?" my best friend whispered.

I wanted to tell her that this was nothing compared to the insanity of the convention (because, for example, I hadn't seen anyone with hats shaped like produce . . . yet), but somehow bringing up Boston didn't seem like a good idea, so instead I just nodded and tried to squeeze through the crowds.

A massive banner (that I'm fairly sure was also bullet-proof) circled the stage, reading WALK THE WALK. I turned and scanned the long stretch of barricades that ran through the center of the crowd. A huge tour bus turned onto the street and stopped at the end of the alleyway that cut through the audience. Its doors swung open, and somewhere in the distance, the Tri-County High School Marching Band started to play as Governor Winters and The Senator stepped out and started down the long promenade full of hands to shake and babies to kiss—two thousand screaming people, any one of whom could have given me the bump on my head.

In my ear I heard a steady stream of unfamiliar voices.

"Sir, could you remove your hands from your pockets, please?" a tall Secret Service agent asked the man behind me.

"Delta team, I don't like the looks of the guy on the library steps. I repeat, the library steps."

Instantly, I felt the entire junior CoveOps class from the

Gallagher Academy for Exceptional Young Women pivot to see a guy in a trench coat approach a man in a plaid shirt and block his view of the candidates, who were passing in the street below them.

A group of women were waving a sign that read GOD BLESS YOU, MACEY AND PRESTON, and as if on cue, Preston ran toward the women and hugged them while, twenty feet away, CNN carried the whole scene live and in color.

But Macey didn't run anywhere. Or hug anyone (which is totally in character anyway—kidnapping attempt or not). Instead she held her father's hand. She waved. She smiled.

"We have to be perfect every second of every day, ladies." I've heard Joe Solomon say some pretty heady stuff in the past two years, but I don't think I'd ever heard him sound more solemn than when he said, "The bad guys just have to get lucky . . . once."

And then I couldn't help it. I thought about Boston. I thought about luck. I thought about how close we came to having a very bad ending to our summer vacation.

"I don't know if any of you will go into protection services someday or not, ladies, but if you do . . ." Mr. Solomon's voice was soft in my ear, steady against the din of Secret Service orders. "This is your worst nightmare."

At that moment, I'm pretty sure Bex wanted to drag our roommate into the nearest bulletproof automobile and drive back to Roseville as quickly as humanly possible. But that wasn't going to happen because 1) the real Secret Service might shoot us if we tried, 2) the CNN correspondents might have some interesting questions if Bex took out Senator McHenry's body men with two well-placed kicks, and 3) our midterm grades were probably riding on doing exactly *not* that, and as if we needed reminding, our teacher's voice was a constant in our ears.

"Given the wind velocity and direction, the greatest threat from sniper assault is where, Ms. Morrison?"

Bex and I looked at each other and mouthed, "The church steeple," just as Mick said those very words.

"Four members of the Secret Service have infiltrated the protesters across the street, Ms. Fetterman," Mr. Solomon asked again. "Identify the agents."

"Uh . . ." Anna started while, on the street in front of us, Aunt Abby and Macey were walking by. "Red backpack," Anna answered. "Lady in the blue bandanna. The man in the yellow T-shirt, and . . ." She trailed off.

"Anyone?" Mr. Solomon asked.

"The guy with the long red beard," I found myself saying. I wasn't sure when I'd even seen him, but as soon as I said the words I knew they were true.

"Why?" Mr. Solomon questioned.

"The static," I said. "Two and a half minutes ago there was a burst of static on the Secret Service frequency. He flinched."

Somewhere in the crowd of bodies, I could have sworn I felt Joe Solomon smile.

* * *

I used to wonder if Secret Service Agents ever got tired of hearing the same speeches from the same people a dozen times a day every day until someone either has to give a speech that says they won or give a speech that says they lost. But after that day I started wondering if the security team even heard the speeches at all.

"Beta team, protesters stay in Level Two. I repeat, protesters stay in Level Two," one of the anonymous voices said.

"Charlie team, we have unusual movement in a window in the City National Bank building," another voice said, and in a flash, all the blinds on the fourth floor of the building across the street were pulled down.

And then . . . a voice I recognized. "Peacock is stage-ready and moving."

"Aunt Abby," I whispered to Bex.

"Peacock?" she whispered back.

Onstage, The Senator was sweeping out his hand and saying, "Family. I don't have to tell the Buckeye state how much family means to me."

The crowd cheered wildly for a few minutes, but when Macey replaced her father at the microphone, a hush fell so completely over the Ohio swing voters that I could have sworn someone or something had turned the volume down.

"It's great being here today." Macey looked out over the crowd. She looked lost for a moment—dazed. But then I could have sworn her gaze fell on Bex and me. A new light seemed to fill her eyes as she looked at us and added, "With my family." At this point Senator McHenry put his arm around his wife, and I couldn't help thinking about Clipboard Lady's direction of "spontaneous hugging."

"And there's something I want to say," Macey went on, even stronger now. "There's nothing we can't do if we stick together. There's nothing we can't overcome if we try. I learned that from the people who love me. The people who know . . . the *real* me." This time I knew Macey was looking straight at us.

Beside me, I heard Bex whisper, "That's our girl."

"Ms. Baxter." Mr. Solomon's voice brought us back to the moment, to the mission. "There's a man thirty feet behind you in a denim jacket. Get his fingerprints without his knowledge." With a wink, Bex was gone.

There were more speeches, more cheering, but eventually Macey walked down the steps on the left side of the stage and through a gap in the bleachers that led to a secure area behind the stands. As soon as she disappeared, I heard my aunt's voice saying, "Peacock is secure and holding in the yellow tent," and I took my first deep breath since Sunday night.

The crowd was staring at the stage while Governor Winters said, "Our opponents have had four years to talk the talk, but now it's time to *walk the walk*!" People clapped. People laughed. It was like he was a puppet master and two thousand people jumped every time he pulled the strings.

But I didn't clap. I didn't laugh. I just kept hearing Mr. Solomon's voice—not in my ear—in my head. I remembered something he'd said in the helicopter. "Protection is ten percent protocol and ninety percent instinct."

And just then my instincts were telling me to turn around. Maybe it was the way the buildings lined the grassy lawn, maybe it was the crowd of people that passed by me, but something made me think about last semester and Washington, D.C. So while The Senator and Governor Winters stood with their hands locked together above their heads, and the band started playing, I turned and watched the crowd clapping and dancing. The candidates pushed toward the barriers, and the crowd rushed closer, but one guy slipped away.

Farther from the bulletproof banner.

Farther from everything.

Except the bleachers and the yellow tent that stood behind them.

Another banner hung from the side of the bleachers, advertising www.winters-mchenry.com, and I watched it blow in the breeze, a corner flapping free, banging against the aluminum posts, but no one noticed the sound. No one saw the gap. No civilian would have appreciated that sliver of access, and what it meant. But the guy in the cap walked toward the banner. He slipped through the tiny crack, and that's when I knew he was a pavement artist.

I knew he was like me.

"No," I felt myself scream; but with the band and the crowd and the chatter of agents securing the rope lines, the word was lost. And he was gone.

I followed, pushing through the gap myself, but all I

could see was litter and the tangled wires and rods of the metal stands.

For such a sunny day, it was dark under the bleachers; for such a screaming crowd, the noise seemed very far away. A warm breeze blew red, white, and blue confetti across my feet, while the band played and the people cheered.

And I felt someone behind me.

And for the second time that month, a strange hand grasped my shoulder.

I forgot all about Mr. Solomon's assignment as I reached back and grabbed the offending hand, stepped into the move, and swung the guy smoothly through the air, watching him crash onto a red balloon with a pop.

But suddenly I was the one who was breathless as I stared down at the guy who lay beneath me, and I heard the only words I totally wasn't prepared to hear.

"Hello, Gallagher Girl."

Chapter twelve

Zach was there. Zach was staring up at me through the shadow of the bleachers, lying on his back, his shoulders pinned beneath my knees.

He was real this time. This wasn't spy genes and teen hormones running away with me. I wasn't hallucinating or daydreaming or the victim of some freaky hologram-based countersurveillance diversion.

I was just looking . . .

At Zach.

"Hey, Gallagher Girl," he said after . . . I don't know . . . an hour or something, "you gonna let me up now?"

But I totally didn't want to let him up because A) I had the superior position, and with any boy—much less a Blackthorne Boy—superior position is something you should hang on to when you get a chance, B) if I didn't let him up, there was a lot less chance of him retaliating by flipping me through the air like a rag doll (which I totally wouldn't have put past him), and C) I kinda liked knowing where I stood with Zach. For once.

So instead of moving aside and pulling him to his feet like a good girl, I just leaned over him like a Gallagher Girl and said, "What are you *doing* here?"

But Zach didn't answer right away. Instead, he did that Zach thing he always did. He gave me a look that was so deep—so intense—that it was as if he were trying to send the answer to me over some cosmic, psychic thread or something.

Then he smirked and said, "I'm *very* interested in Ohio politics."

I scooted backward, stumbling to my feet as I blurted, "You can't vote."

"Yeah, but I can campaign." He pointed to the WINTERS–MCHENRY button on his jacket as if to prove his point. And then it hit me—the feelings of panic that cute boys and kidnapping attempts have probably been prompting inside Gallagher Girls for a hundred years.

I'd thought about seeing him about a billion times. I'd imagined what I'd be wearing and what cool thing I would say, but I can assure you that in none of my fantasies had I been wearing my most uncomfortable jeans and a T-shirt that was two sizes too large. I'd thought about what kind of girl I was going to be—interested but indifferent, lovely but amused. And yet I was none of those things as I looked down at him and muttered, "You're a long way from Blackthorne."

"Yeah." He smiled. "Well, I heard that Macey McHenry was going to be making her first post-convention public appearance here today"—he stood and brushed some stray confetti from my hair—"and where there's one Gallagher Girl, there are usually others."

His smile deepened, and at that moment I seriously thought I would scream (but for a totally different reason.)

"We're like smoke and fire that way," I stuttered, trying my best to act cooler than I felt.

He smiled his slow, knowing smile. "Something like that."

And then a whole new kind of panic hit me—ZACH WAS THERE! Because he knew Macey was going to be there? And because he thought *I* might be with Macey?

(Note to self: Modify Liz's boy-to-English translator to account for multiple interpretations at once!)

That couldn't be it—could it? Was it possible that Zachary Goode had broken out of his top-secret spy school because this was his first chance at seeing me outside of *my* top secret spy school?

Oh.

My.

Gosh.

Could I go back to battling rooftop attackers now? Because at least with rooftop attackers you know where you stand! But boys—especially *that boy*—seemed to always be a mystery.

I heard the crowd erupt into applause again as the

governor continued his speech, but it felt like all of that was taking place on the other side of the earth.

"I thought you'd vowed to stay out of secret passageways and laundry chutes, but I guess . . ." he started but didn't finish. Instead he reached up and traced the bruise that had all but faded along my hairline, and I felt something that has absolutely nothing to do with blunt force trauma.

And then something dawned on me. "How did you know about the laundry chute?"

Zach took a deep breath then smiled and pointed to himself like he used to do and said, "Spy."

I heard a voice in my earpiece say, "Chameleon, I know you're being Chameleony, but if you could wave or something, or tell me where you are, that would be great."

"Bleachers," I told her.

"Bex?" Zach guessed.

"Yeah," I answered.

"So you've got backup?" It was a truly weird question in what was shaping up to be a truly weird day, so for a second I just stood there, wondering if he was asking me as a boy or if he was asking as a spy. "The girls are here? And Solomon?"

"Of course they are."

But then one of the hundreds of voices in my ear was saying "Alpha team, there's movement under the bleachers," and in a flash I moved.

"Zach, there's someone under—"

I stopped. I realized *we* were the people under the bleachers.

"You!" one of the agents called. But as I spun to face him, his right hand, which had been inching toward where his regulation sidearm was holstered, relaxed. He almost smiled. And maybe for the first time ever I realized how totally advantageous being a sixteen-year-old girl can be.

"Miss," the agent said, "this area is restricted. I'm going to have to ask you to go back behind the barricades."

"Oh my gosh," I said, sounding a tad bit ditzier than my IQ might suggest. "I had to go to the bathroom *so bad*, so we—"

"We?" the agent said, going on alert again. He scanned the area. Big men in dark suits appeared out of nowhere. The earpiece was alive with chatter and commands.

"I was . . ." I started, the words coming harder now. And still I kept turning and looking.

But Zach was already gone.

Chapter Thirteen

"Yeah, we were looking for a bathroom." A voice came slicing through the barricade of agents in dark suits that surrounded me. Even though Secret Service agents are notoriously smart and incredibly well trained, everyone around me seemed to cower at the sight of Macey McHenry.

I watched my roommate turn to the agents and summon her inner Gallagher Girl (the snobby kind). "Do you have a problem with that?"

And that's how a chameleon was saved by a peacock.

"Thanks, boys," Aunt Abby said, appearing at Macey's side. "I think we can take it from here."

As dark suits scattered, my aunt took me by the arm and led me out from under the bleachers and into the sun of the main staging area while she softly sang, *"I'm gonna tell your mother."*

"I'm sorry, Aunt Abby," I told her. "I just"—I thought about Zach . . . mysterious Zach . . . suddenly disappearing

Zach—"saw something," I said—not some*one*.

But my aunt was shaking her head. "I don't even want to know how you got back here." She stopped. "Wait, you'd better tell me how you got back here."

After I explained, she walked twenty feet to where a security detail stood around a row of dark Suburbans.

"Emergency extraction vehicles," I said, turning to Macey, who was too busy staring at my feet to marvel at any of the totally cool surveillance things going on around us.

"I'll give you five hundred dollars if you trade me shoes," Macey said. I looked down at the pumps her mother had no doubt forced her into, and I totally knew she wasn't joking. But you can't put a price on comfort (as all pavement artists know), so I pretended like I didn't hear her, which wasn't all that hard considering that I absolutely had *other* things on my mind!

Zach had come to the rally! To see *me*?

"Macey, you're never going to believe who I just—"

"Hey," a voice cut me off. "I know you!"

I recognized the voice, but more than that I recognized the look on Macey's face as Preston came into view.

"Don't you have a baby to kiss?" Macey said with a sigh.

"Cammie, right?" Preston asked. "Macey didn't tell me you were coming."

"Yeah. It's a great chance to see the political process up close and—"

"Seriously," Macey snapped. "Go. Kiss. A baby."

"Can you believe her?" Preston asked, cocking his head

toward Macey. "Every time she sees me, all she does is call me baby and talk about kissing."

Macey looked like she kind of wanted to kill him. But I kind of wanted to laugh.

Maybe it was just that I had boys on the brain. Maybe it was the relief of knowing, for the time being, that Macey was okay. But at that moment Preston seemed kind of . . .

Hot?

No. No way, I told myself. And then I looked at Macey, who hated being in uncomfortable shoes and at her parents' disposal, and I thought that maybe Preston Winters was the one person who might hate all those things as much as she did. And as every spy knows, common enemies are how allies always begin.

"So hey," Preston said softly.

A gospel choir was singing in the distance. The Secret Service was getting ready for the long walk back to the busses. But Preston didn't seem to notice; he didn't seem to care. He seemed totally immune to those prying eyes and listening ears as he leaned closer and said, "I'm really glad I saw you."

Oh my gosh, I thought. Is it possible that *two* boys are flirting with me within ten minutes of each other?

But it wasn't flirting.

It was worse.

Totally, infinitely, utterly worse, because while the gospel band stopped singing and some military planes flew overhead, Preston looked at me as if he were really *seeing* me and said, "I wanted to thank you . . . for Boston."

The girl in me started to exhale just as the spy in me studied the change in his breathing pattern and the dilatation of his eyes. I was seriously beginning to panic as he said, "That was really . . . awesome of you."

"Oh, it was nothing!" I blurted.

"Cammie's always doing stuff like that," Macey said, hearing my unease. "She's a total Girl Scout."

"Well, whatever she is," he said, turning to Macey, "it looked like you were one too."

As Macey glanced at me, I knew that neither of us wanted to imagine what might happen if the potential first son thought too hard or too long about what he'd seen on that rooftop.

"I was so freaked out," Preston said. "But you two, you were . . . *rational.*"

"So, Macey," I said loudly, "I really enjoyed your speech."

"I mean"—Preston went on as if I wasn't even standing there . . . as if *he* wasn't standing there. Instead he stared into space as if the movie of what had happened in Boston was playing in his mind—"there were, what? Ten guys after us?"

"Two men. One woman," Macey and I corrected him at exactly the same time.

"And you guys were . . ." He looked at us as if he were seeing us for the first time. "You're *girls!*" he blurted as if the fact had totally eluded him until then.

"Thanks for noticing," Macey said, grabbing my arm and pulling me away.

Preston followed after. "But you held your own against like a dozen—"

"Three!" Macey and I corrected him again.

"Men." He stopped in front of us, blocking our path. Which meant that unless we wanted to impress him with our unusual physical abilities even more, we were probably going to have to wait him out.

Just when I thought things couldn't get worse, he looked right at Macey. "How much do you weigh?"

"Hey!" I blurted, stepping between them. "It was nothing. Really! It was like those women who lift trucks off their babies—that's how I felt." I tried to sound like that moment was as exciting and adrenaline-filled and foreign to me as it had been for him.

"Yeah," Macey added.

"But the moves . . ." he started.

"My mom made me take a self-defense class," I blurted. (Totally not a lie.)

"Wow." He nodded. "Hope you got extra credit."

"I did," I said. (Also *not* a lie.)

"Well . . ." Preston ran his hand through his hair and straightened his tie. "They must be teaching you something special in that school of yours."

Macey and I looked at each other as if we knew we *could* kill him, but getting away might be way more difficult than usual.

And then he laughed.

And we breathed.

And he looked at both of us with (if he hadn't been a politician's son and all) an expression of genuine gratitude as he said, "I'm just glad I get to do this with girls like you."

"Mr. Winters!" one of the agents called. "We're moving."

A team of agents surrounded him, ushering Preston away, but Macey lingered a second longer.

"Well, he seemed . . . nice?" I finally found the strength to mutter.

But Macey merely looked at me. "You're a spy, Cam. Don't you know that nothing is ever as it seems?"

I didn't get to mention Zach. I didn't get to tell her what I thought of her speech. I didn't even get to ask Aunt Abby if she was really serious about telling my mom that I'd been caught out-of-bounds.

Instead I watched the Secret Service swarm around my roommate once again. A gate swung open and Macey stepped toward her parents. Her father reached out for her hand, but she was already waving, pulling in votes and smiles and handshakes.

And there was already a voice in my earpiece telling me it was time to go home.

Chapter fourteen

Do you know how long it took to get back to school? One hundred and seventy-two minutes. Do you know how long it took for things to return to normal? Well . . . I guess I'm still kind of waiting.

As soon as we got back, Mr. Solomon dragged us all the way down to Sublevel Two to review surveillance tapes and take a pop quiz. (I scored a 98%.) By the time we got upstairs to the foyer I heard the scraping of forks and the clanking of ice in our second-best crystal, but I totally wasn't hungry, especially when I saw Macey walking through the front door.

"Macey!" I yelled.

"Cam." Bex and Liz ran behind me. "What's going on?"

It was a normal night at a very abnormal school. But even by Gallagher Academy standards I'd had a very exceptional day, so I raced through the entry hall and climbed the stairs, still calling, "Macey!"

By the time I caught up to her she had already taken off

her jacket and was standing there in a silk blouse. She was carrying a string of pearls and had crammed the scarf she'd been wearing at the rally into her purse. With every step, Macey was shedding her fake facade—her cover—one piece of pocket litter at a time.

"You're back," I said.

"Yeah," she said in the tone of the incredibly tired, "very observant. Hey, what was up with you today?" She took another step, then shed another piece of the clothing that only a mother can love. "When I saw you, you looked kind of . . . freaked?"

"Wait," Bex said, "you *saw* her?"

"Yeah, I was going to tell you, but well . . . we haven't exactly had a moment . . . And it's not exactly something you . . . And I just didn't know how . . . And—"

"Cammie." Bex snapped me out of it. She crossed her arms, stared me down, and gave me that "you've got some explaining to do" look that I've come to love. And fear. (Well, mostly fear.) And I knew I couldn't keep my secret any longer.

"I saw something!" I blurted. Then I had to correct myself as I said, *"Someone."*

The halls were quiet around us. Dark. The days were getting shorter. Summer was finally gone. And maybe that was why I shivered as I said, "Zach."

Time it took me to tell the whole story: twenty-two minutes and forty-seven seconds.

Time it would have taken me to tell the story had I not been constantly interrupted: two minutes and forty-six seconds.

Number of times Liz said, "No way!": thirty-three.

Number of times Bex gave me her "You could have brought me with you" look: nine.

"But what was he *doing* there?" Liz was asking again (time number seven, to be exact).

"I don't know," I managed to mutter. "I mean, one minute I'm thinking he's breaching security—well, technically, he *did* breach security . . ." I trailed off. "And the next I'm flipping him to the ground and—"

"Staring deeply into his eyes?" Liz guessed, because while security breaches might be serious, eye-staring-into is something that should *never* be ignored.

"Maybe Blackthorne was there for an assignment too?" Bex asked.

"Maybe," I said, but my heart wasn't in it. I thought about his cryptic postcard—his warning—and the way he'd looked at me that day. "It's just that something about him seemed . . . different."

"What?" Bex said. I could feel her moving toward me. Like a tiger. She was lethal and beautiful and very, very cat-like in the curiosity department. "What are you thinking about?"

I didn't know what was more concerning—that there had been a gap, however small, in Macey's security perimeter, or that Zach had slipped through it.

I thought about the boy who had kissed me last spring

and the one who had looked at me under the bleachers. "He seemed"—I started slowly, still trying to put the pieces together—"worried."

"Ooh!" Liz squealed. "He wants to protect you!"

"I don't need protecting," I told her, but Liz only shrugged.

"It's the thought that counts."

"Well, there is *another* option," Bex said, with a very mischievous grin. "Maybe he went under the bleachers knowing you wouldn't be able to resist *following him* under the bleachers. . . ."

She let her voice trail off as she stared at me, the possibilities lingering until Liz felt the need to blurt: "So you could be alone!"

Okay, I don't want to sound braggy. Or unprofessional. Or naïve. But is it wrong to admit that I'd been kind of hoping all day that was the reason? (Partly because, as a girl, that's a good reason, and as a spy, it meant he wasn't conspiring to commit high treason.)

"No," I blurted. "No. That can't be possible. He wouldn't leave school and go all the way to Cleveland and sneak into a restricted area and everything just to see . . . me." I turned to Macey, our resident expert on all things *boy*. "Would he?"

"Don't look at me," Macey said, waving her hands (which were, by that time, holding a pump, a jacket, and a "walk the walk" campaign button). "I have a whole other kind of boy problem."

Wait. MACEY McHENRY HAD A BOY PROBLEM? I couldn't be sure I'd heard correctly, and evidently I wasn't alone.

"Boy"—Liz stammered—"problem. YOU?"

Macey rolled her eyes. "Not *that* kind of problem. Preston."

"Oh," Liz said, sounding way too matchmakery, if you want to know the truth. "He is kind of cute. And really socially aware. You know, I read this article in—"

"He's a dork," Macey said, cutting her off.

"But you have so much in common," Liz protested. Macey glared. "I mean, besides the dork thing."

"'Common' is overrated," Macey said with another sigh.

"Well then," Liz said, "what's the problem?"

"The problem is that we were attacked by three highly trained operatives and lived to tell the tale," I said without even realizing that I'd known the answer all along.

"Bingo," Macey said. "And Preston was impressed. Very impressed."

"So boys really *do* make passes at girls who kick—"

"Bex!" I cut my best friend off.

Can I just say that it's really pretty hard to deal with boys who may want to . . .

A. Date you, or

B. Kill you, or

C. Learn the origins of your freaklike self-defense capabilities!

And that day it was highly possible that we might have been dealing with ALL THREE!

Will the boy drama in my life ever go away?! Seriously. I'm asking.

"Even after you left, he wouldn't shut up about it," Macey told me.

"You could have shut him up," Bex suggested.

"Don't think I wasn't tempted."

A group of eighth graders passed by, singing at the top of their lungs, but the four of us stayed quiet and still inside the dark alcove.

"You're smiling," Macey blurted, no doubt accusing Bex of doing something Bexish. "*Why* are you smiling?"

"Nothing," Bex said with a shake of her head. "I just keep thinking . . ."

Bex isn't one for trailing off. She always knows what comes next and never starts what she can't finish. So maybe it was that fact, or the way the smile faded from her face, but something made me hold my breath as she found the words to say, "I just keep thinking how shocked they must have been. You know . . . *them*. They thought they were coming after a girl. But instead they got . . ."

"Gallagher Girls," Liz finished for her.

The two of them smiled at each other. But Macey and I—we just stared through the shadows, a new realization dawning on both of us as I said, "But they *weren't* surprised."

Chapter fifteen

I've told the story here; I don't want to tell it again. This is my official record—hopefully the last time I'll have to answer the question, "So what happened last summer in Boston?"

I've told it now so many times that it comes out automatically, like a textbook I've memorized, like a song stuck in my head.

But after that . . .

After that the story changed.

The facts were still the same—I'd remembered them correctly all along. But I understood something else then. When the film played in my mind I didn't focus on the hits or the kicks. That night I saw the eyes, the way arms were ready to parry our punches. The way no one seemed shocked as Macey performed a textbook Malinowski Maneuver on a guy twice her size.

A spy is only as good as her cover—as her legend. The

bad guys weren't supposed to know the truth about us.

But they did.

"You're sure," Bex asked me. Again. We huddled together in the nearest, quietest, safest place I could find, surrounded by the remnants of the first-ever covert carrier pigeon breeding program. Liz sat on an overturned pigeon coop. A soft wind blew through the open gaps in the wall, which looked out into the night.

Roseville was just two miles away. And Josh. And normalcy. But somehow my first boyfriend and his perfectly ordinary life seemed like a different world entirely as I looked at Bex and then at Liz and, finally, at Macey.

"They really weren't surprised," Macey said again, almost laughing now. She looked at me. "Why didn't we see that?"

It was as if we'd both missed an easy question on a pop quiz and Macey couldn't help having a good laugh at our stupidity.

"So . . ." Bex spoke slowly, carefully. "They know."

She looked out the glassless windows as if *they* might have been out there even as we spoke, because if they knew who we were . . . they knew where we lived.

"But that can't be," Liz protested. "No one knows the truth about the Gallagher Academy."

But I just followed Bex's gaze into the darkness and thought about another night in another room, when Zach had asked me about the mystery surrounding my father's death. I found his words coming back to me as I wrapped my arms around myself and whispered, "Somebody knows."

"So they knew Macey would have training, and they came after her and Preston anyway?" Liz asked.

I saw my best friends looking at me—and even in the dark I couldn't hide the truth any longer.

"Well . . ." I started slowly, "on the roof, Preston was with us."

"Yeah," Bex said. I could feel her impatience building, so I spoke faster.

"I got him out of there—got him off of that roof—and they didn't really . . . care."

"What do you mean, Cam?" Liz asked.

"She means they didn't want him," Macey said. "They didn't want us," she added, growing stronger. And then she stopped. She shrugged. "They wanted *me*."

I'd been fearing that moment for days, thinking about the girl at the lake. I'd worried what the knowledge might do to her—to us. But from the time she'd stepped foot out of her parents' limousine, Macey had been a surprise, and this was no exception.

She squinted at me. She shook her head. It was the exact same look she got when she mastered a formula for Mr. Mosckowitz's class, as if things were finally starting to make sense.

"I'm gonna get my mom and Aunt Abby." I started for the door, but then Macey spoke.

"You think they don't know already?"

And it hit me—the truth. Of course they knew. They'd *always* known.

"So either they came after Macey in spite of her training . . ." Liz started.

"Or because of it," Bex replied.

But the strangest thing was happening. The moon was rising, full and clear. The lights of Roseville shone in the distance. Everything felt alive again, and I could see that in Macey. It was as if she knew it wasn't random anymore—there was purpose. And that made all the difference.

"So I guess the question is," Bex said, crossing her arms, "what are we gonna do about it?"

Covert Operations Report
By Cameron Morgan, Macey McHenry, Elizabeth Sutton, and Rebecca Baxter (hereafter referred to as "The Operatives")

During a routine civilian engagement, Operatives McHenry and Morgan were attacked by figures representing an unknown organization with unknown affiliations and unknown goals.

After two weeks of extensive research (and some particularly fine computer hacking by agent Sutton), The Operatives learned the following:

There are no fewer than two dozen international lawsuits filed against McHenry Cosmetics (even though the Eye

Rejuvenation cream clearly states on the label that temporary blindness is a possible side effect).

Much to Macey's shock, Senator McHenry does not appear to have any illegitimate children (that The Operatives know about).

No one holding a significant amount of stock in Macey's mom's company made a significant gamble that the price of the stock would go down following the kidnapping attempt.

The McHenry family has approximately seventy-six disgruntled former servants (of whom, Macey swears, only seventy-five have cause to be really, truly angry).

It's easy to imagine that a family of spies would have a lot of enemies. Well, turns out we've got nothing on politicians and people who manufacture semi-dangerous cosmetics. By the time we'd run down every shady business deal and political scandal, the list of suspects was long—like, the number of digits of pi that Liz knows by heart, long—and I wasn't sleeping any easier.

"It's impossible," I told Bex one day in P&E, but Bex, sadly, misunderstood, because instead of commiserating, she grabbed my arm and executed the most perfect Axley Maneuver I'd ever seen.

"Ow," I said, looking up at her. But Bex just laughed.

"Wuss," she said, then stepped back to illustrate. "It's not impossible. All you have to do is shift your weight in a counter—"

"Not the move," I snapped as I climbed to my feet, shifted my weight, and showed her. "Macey," I whispered as she landed on the mat.

"Oh," Bex said, staring up at me.

Outside, the first hints of color were appearing on the trees, and the wind was growing cooler. Fall was coming soon, and yet the mysteries of summer were still alive and well.

"I touched them, Bex," I said, my voice low against the steady din of grunts and kicks that filled the loft. My breath came harder. "I heard their voices and smelled their breath and I can't tell you anything about them except . . ." I trailed off. But Bex, who is excellent in both the spy and best friend departments, read my mind. "It's the ring, isn't it?"

Beads of sweat ran from my forehead to my chin, but I didn't wipe them away. "I've seen that emblem somewhere before."

"I believe you, Cam," Bex started slowly. "But didn't you sketch it for Liz and have her run it through the CIA database?"

"Yes."

"And if they are as good as you say, then do you really think that woman would wear a ring that could lead us to her? It's a mistake," Bex finished, and I just stood there, the unspoken truth settling around us: they didn't make mistakes.

"Morgan!" our teacher called. "Baxter! Back to work, please."

I pulled Bex to her feet.

"You know," Bex said, "there is one resource we haven't utilized yet."

Through the window, I saw my mother crossing the grounds.

"No!" I snapped as Bex lunged toward me, her foot sailing far too close to my ear for comfort. "I am not spying on my mom again," I said, maybe too loudly considering that Tina Walters and Eva Alvarez were ten feet away.

"Who said anything about your mom?" Bex whispered to me, gesturing behind us at the rock wall and Mr. Solomon.

"No way," I whispered. "Mom was bad enough, but Mr. Solomon would be—"

"Look again," she whispered.

And then I saw that Mr. Solomon was not alone. That he was with someone. That he was smiling. That they were laughing.

And that my best friend in the world thought that I should snoop on my aunt Abby.

I would like to point out that, despite evidence to the contrary, I don't like breaking rules. I do not enjoy violating people's privacy—especially people I love. And I try to never, ever stick my nose into other people's business. Still, I couldn't shake the feeling that what was happening with Macey had become my business when I fell forty feet through a metal shaft and landed in a cart full of dirty laundry.

So that's why we huddled in our suite that Thursday night.

And that's why I didn't protest as Bex asked, "So, everyone clear?"

Macey laced up her running shoes and Liz gripped her flashlight, while I just sat there telling myself that there's a big difference between spying and snooping, and espionage isn't so much about uncovering embarrassing things as it is, you know, about saving lives (and other important stuff).

Macey was safe. The Secret Service and Aunt Abby were on the case. But if someone was hunting Gallagher Girls, then none of us would rest until we knew who. And why.

Covert Operations Report
PHASE ONE
1830 hours

On the night of October 1, Operative McHenry announced to the entire post-dinner crowd in the Grand Hall that she was going for a run in the woods.

Agent Abigail Cameron announced that the protectee wasn't allowed in the woods alone, and that Agent Cameron had a headache, so therefore, the proctectee wasn't going anywhere.

Operative McHenry (a.k.a., the proctectee) announced that she was going for a run and if Agent Cameron didn't like it she could . . . (Well, let's just say it was in Arabic. And it wasn't very ladylike.)

Agent Cameron announced (louder, and in Farsi)

that the protectee was not to leave the mansion.

Operative McHenry replied (even louder) that she WAS.

And then she fled the Grand Hall. Fast.

Agent Cameron had no choice but to follow.

Walking through the mansion with Bex that night, I felt a little sick to my stomach—not because of what we were about to do, but because I was afraid it might actually work. I might learn something I couldn't unlearn. And every spy knows that we live our lives on a need-to-know basis for a reason.

I glanced out the window and saw a blur as Macey dashed through the woods, Abby following closely behind her. From behind a tree, a flashlight clicked off and on twice, Liz's way of telling us the coast was clear. Everything was going according to plan, and yet a nervous feeling settled in as I walked toward my aunt's room and knocked, knowing full well that no one would answer.

It took ten full minutes to break into Aunt Abby's room. Yes, ten minutes. Not necessarily because my aunt had used every surveillance detection known to man, but because we couldn't be sure she hadn't, and Bex and I weren't taking any chances. (We were juniors, after all!)

When we finally stepped into Abby's room, for some reason I held my breath. Our flashlights played over a closetful of clothes I'd never seen my aunt wear. There was a dresser covered with knickknacks, trinkets from other worlds and other times, and there wasn't a doubt in my mind that each one held a story that I'd never heard. I'd been listening to her wild tales for weeks, but every spy learns early on that the stories that matter most are the ones that you don't tell.

Abby had come back to us—but one look around her room told me that a part of her was still long gone.

The beam of my flashlight nearly blinded me as it shone against the mirror. A tiny black-and-white photo was tacked to the bottom corner of the glass. I stood there for a long time staring at the image of my aunt, my favorite teacher, and my father—all three laughing at a joke that was long since over.

For a second I almost forgot what we were searching for. Someone was after Macey, but right then my aunt was the mystery I most wanted to solve.

"Cam."

Bex's voice cut through the darkness as the beam of her flashlight fell upon—an image I'd hoped I'd never see again.

"That's it," I muttered, stepping closer to look at the grainy black-and-white photograph—a close-up of a hand. It was pretty good considering it had been taken with an NSA satellite a few hundred miles above the earth. It didn't show the faces. If I hadn't known, I wouldn't have even recognized my own shoulder and neck. But the hand was fully in focus, the ring as clear as day.

"Do you recognize it?" I asked, feeling my heart beat faster, seeing the proof at last that I wasn't chasing a phantom image from my mind.

Bex stared harder. "Maybe," she said, then shook her head. "I don't know."

1830 hours

Agent Cameron succeeded in dragging Operative McHenry back to the primary mansion.

Unfortunately, Operatives Morgan and Baxter had no way of knowing that.

"Oh, Joe!" Abby's voice echoed down the hallway. "You are going to get me into so much trouble."

I froze, totally unsure what was more terrifying: the look on Bex's face or the flirty tone of my aunt's laugh or the sound of a key being inserted into the lock on Abby's door.

I didn't have a clue what to do. I mean, as a rule, hiding is never a very good idea. When in doubt, get out, Mr. Solomon always says. But I wasn't exactly sure what he'd say when he is the person who is about to catch you.

"Bed!" I snapped, grabbing Bex by the back of the neck. "Now!"

Crawling underneath Aunt Abby's bed, I couldn't help but think about the thousands of times in the past four and a half years when I'd wondered where she was and what she was doing. (Note to self: be very, very careful what you wish for.)

"Oh, Joe, stop!" my aunt cried as the door creaked open. "What if Rachel found out? She'd never forgive me."

125

In the darkness under the bed, Bex looked at me, her eyes as wide and bright as the moon, as she mouthed the word, "Solomon!"

I wanted to put my hands in my ears and sing. I wanted to wish myself into another room—another galaxy—but instead I just squeezed my eyes together.

And that's probably why I didn't see the bedskirt fly up and two hands grab my ankles.

My back skidded on the hardwood floors as a great force jerked me from my hiding place.

My aunt stared down and said, "Hey, squirt."

The good news was that Mr. Solomon was nowhere to be found. The bad news was that my aunt had had absolutely no trouble finding *us*.

"Bex, darling, could you give us a minute?"

Bex looked at me. One of the cardinal rules of being a Gallagher Girl was simple: never leave your sister behind. But this was different, and we both knew it.

"See you upstairs," I said as she walked away.

The door closed behind her, and Abby turned to me. "You really have grown up."

"Aunt Abby," I hurried with the words, "I'm—"

I had intended to say "sorry" but Abby finished for me. "Busted."

She dropped onto the bed and pulled off a black (standard Secret Service-issue) loafer that was covered with mud.

I looked around the room. "Uh . . . where's Mr. Solomon?"

"Heck if I know." Abby shrugged. She must have read my confused expression because then she added, "Oh, Joe," mimicking her earlier tone. She laughed. "Squirt, you should have seen the look on your face."

"Was I that obvious?" I asked.

"Oh, no way," Abby said, and as crazy as it might sound, I felt a little proud. "But the bed thing is kind of a Morgan family tradition."

"Why? Did my mom—"

"Oh, not your mom." Abby stopped me. She cocked an eyebrow. "Your dad."

Your dad, she'd said. She'd just . . . volunteered it. My father was always with my mother and me, and yet neither of us ever said his name. I realized then that Dad was like a ghost that only Aunt Abby didn't fear. She walked to the dresser and pulled out a bag of M&M's.

"Want one?" she asked, offering me the bag. For a second I thought about the first time I'd met Zach, but the thought quickly vanished.

"Gosh, your dad loved sweets!" she exclaimed as she sank onto the bed. "You get that from him, you know. I remember this one time, we were trailing this double agent through a bazaar in Athens, and there was this lady selling chocolates. And they looked so good. And I could see your dad, and it was all he could do to keep his eye on the subject. But your dad was a pavement artist—you know that, right? So he's following this guy, while I'm up on this second-story balcony getting the whole thing on surveillance and routing it back to Langley. And your dad's a pro, but I could tell that he wanted something sweet so bad he could hardly stand it. The only problem was . . ."

I watched my aunt carry on. There was a light in her eyes, an easiness to her words that I don't think I'd ever heard before. It was just another funny story, an entertaining tale. I mean, sure it was classified and dangerous and she might have been violating about a dozen CIA bylaws by telling me, but still she talked, and I listened.

"Here's the thing you've got to know," she said as she leaned closer. "Everything's so crowded that if you blinked at the wrong time you could lose someone, so it's a tough tail, you know? And I'm up on this balcony, but housekeeping wants to come in and clean the room. This maid is yelling, and I'm calling back, and I look away for—I don't know— two seconds. Seriously. No way was it longer than that. And when I look back, your dad's got chocolate on one side of his face and he's smiling at me."

Abby threw her head back, and a part of me wanted to laugh alongside her. I tried to imagine my father alive and half a world away. But the other part of me wanted to cry.

"To this day I don't know how he did it. I went back and looked at the tapes, too." She wiped her hands together as if shaking off the dust of some old mystery she'd given up on solving. "Not a sign of it." Then she looked at me anew. "He was that good."

She pushed herself back onto the bed and told me, "*You're* that good." The way she looked at me said she wasn't speaking as an aunt, she was speaking as a spy.

But I didn't want to be compared to my father in that place. In that way. I didn't deserve it, so I said, "I'm not."

"Yeah, maybe you aren't," Abby said, and despite my protest, a wave of hurt ran through me. But then she cocked an eyebrow. "But you will be."

A new feeling coursed through me—relief. I felt . . . like a girl. Like I didn't know all the answers and that was okay because I still had time to learn them.

"So you're not going to tell my mom?"

"Why?" Abby looked at me. "So she can get mad at both of us?"

It seemed like a fair point until I realized . . .

"But why would she get mad at you?"

"For showing you this." The sound of a heavy notebook dropping onto her wooden dresser caught me off guard. Sheets of paper almost seemed to whistle as she thumbed through the pages.

"The threat book," my aunt told me as I looked at the book. The covers could barely contain it. "This is just this month. This is just Macey—not even counting the rest of the McHenry family." She thumbed through the pages, but I didn't dare to read the words. "We keep copies of every letter, every e-mail, every 911 call and crazy floral delivery card. We keep track of everything, Cam, and analyze it and study it and do what it is we do."

She thumbed through the thick book one final time as she said again, "This is *just this month*."

Every spy knows that what you don't say is just as important—maybe more so—than what you do. Aunt Abby didn't tell me that what was going on was bigger than four Gallagher Girls in training and a secret room. She didn't tell me that there were a whole lot of psycho people in this world, and a whole lot of them were fascinated by one of my best friends. But those were maybe the only things I was sure of as I stepped toward the door.

Still, there was one thing I had to ask.

"What's this symbol?" I asked, pointing to the satellite photo of the hand, which had fallen to the floor. My aunt casually glanced my way.

"Not sure. That's one of the leads we're tracking down. It's probably nothing, though. They were too good to make a mistake that could lead us to them."

"That's what Bex says."

"Bex is good."

"Yeah," I said, turning to leave. Then I stopped. "I've seen it before . . . before Boston."

"You remember where?" Abby asked. A new light filled her eyes, and I got the feeling we were playing a game of covert chicken, both of us waiting to see if the other would blink first.

"It'll come to me," I said, which didn't exactly answer her question, but that's okay. I got the impression that it didn't exactly matter.

"If you remember, let me know," she said, and I would have bet the farm (or . . . well . . . Grandma and Grandpa's farm) that she already knew. I was halfway to the door when she called, "Cam." She held out a piece of paper. "Since you're here, would you mind giving this to Macey?"

I stood in the hall for a long time, reading the first line over and over, wishing the note were written on Evapopaper, trying to find a way to make the words dissolve.

Itinerary: Saturday, 5:00 a.m. Peacock departs Gallagher Academy for Philadelphia, PA.

Things You Can Do When the Life of One of Your Best Friends May Be at Risk, and She's Got to Help Her Dad Campaign for Vice President Anyway, and You Really, Really Don't Want Her to Go:

1. Sweet-talk Mr. Mosckowitz into moving up the exercise where the ninth graders (the grade Macey was up to now) are locked in a room and can't get out until they break the Epstein Equation.

2. Hack into Secret Service databases, leaving indications that the aforementioned roommate had been making some incredibly dangerous threats against another protectee, Preston Winters (because she totally had).

3. If the roommate were to have an allergic reaction to her mother's experimental night cream,

resulting in a terrible zit outbreak that leaves her very unphotogenic and unlikely to test well with undecided women between the ages of 21 and 42 in the process, then maybe she wouldn't be required on the campaign trail after all!

4. Two words: food poisoning (but only as a last resort).

They really were good plans. After all, Bex and I hadn't just aced Mr. Solomon's Logistical Thinking and Planning for Success midterm for nothing. Logistically speaking, we'd been about as covert as we could possibly be without coming right out and hog-tying Macey to her desk chair (a plan that Bex proposed frequently).

But Mr. Mosckowitz wasn't doing the locked room assignment this year, since he'd developed a case of claustrophobia after a top-secret summer assignment that involved a Porta Potti and two Lebanese hairdressers.

And it turns out the Secret Service doesn't take death threats *by* protectees all that seriously. Especially if they're girls. Even if they're Gallagher Girls.

And we should have known that Macey would never get a pimple. Ever. It goes against the laws of nature or something.

And worst of all, the last part of our master plan didn't work because a person can't possibly get food poisoning if the person no longer eats food.

I didn't know if it was nerves or fear or if she really was reverting back to the Macey she had been when she came to us a year before, but night after night we sat at the juniors' table in the Grand Hall while our roommate pushed the food around on her plate—not eating, not laughing. Just waiting for whatever would come next.

"This is bad," Liz said Friday morning as we left Culture and Assimilation. The halls were filling up. And time was running out.

"We could always—"

"No!" Liz and I both snapped, not really thinking that was the time or place to be reminded of Bex's "no one can get out of my slipknots" argument, but it was Macey who made us stop.

"It's okay, guys," Macey said. She turned toward Dr. Fibs's basement lab. "Thanks for trying and everything, but I've got to go." The way she said it, I knew that getting her out of her trip wasn't really up for debate. She shrugged and added, "It's the job."

I might have argued; I might have pleaded, but right then I realized that Bex and I weren't the only ones who had been born into a family business—a genetic fate. Macey's first full sentence had been "Vote for Daddy," and not even a kidnapping attempt, midterms, and the three of us could keep her off the campaign trail.

As Bex pulled me toward the elevator and Sublevel Two, the chaos of the halls faded away, replaced by the smooth whirring of the elevator and the lasers and the sounds of a new set of worries in my head.

"What?" Bex asked.

"Zach," I said numbly.

"Cam, he *is* bloody dreamy—I'm not going to deny you that—but I don't think boys are really the most important thing right now."

"Zach got through."

I thought about him standing behind the bleachers. I thought about *me* standing behind the bleachers. In the restricted zone. "Zach got through security. If he did . . ." I trailed off, not wanting to say the worst of what was on my mind. Bex nodded, not wanting to hear it.

A moment later we were stepping out of the elevator. Our footsteps echoed as we ran, around and around and around the spiraling ramp, lower into the depths of the school.

"Don't worry, Cam," Bex said, not even close to being winded. "We'll think of something. If Mr. Solomon doesn't kill us for being late."

But then she stopped. Partly, I think, because we'd finally reached the classroom; partly because our teacher— perhaps our *best* teacher, our *strictest* teacher—was nowhere to be seen.

I don't know how normal girls behave when a teacher is out of the room, but Gallagher Girls get quiet. Crazy quiet. Because operatives in training learn very early on that you can never really trust that you're alone.

So Bex didn't say anything. I didn't say anything. Even Tina Walters was speechless.

"You're the juniors?"

The voice was one I didn't know. I turned to see a face I didn't recognize. A man. An older man in a Gallagher Academy maintenance department uniform. His name badge read "Art," and he was glaring at us as if he knew we were personally responsible for the terrible hydrochloric acid spill in Dr. Fibs's lab, which had probably taken weeks to clean up.

"Solomon said you were the juniors," Art told us.

"Yes, sir," Mick said, because 1) We've all been taking culture class since we were in the seventh grade and Madame Dabney does her job well, and 2) at the Gallagher Academy, everyone is more than they appear.

We look like normal girls, but we're not. Our teachers could blend in with any prep school faculty in the world, but they're so much more. Every girl in that room knew that to spend your retirement in the Gallagher Academy maintenance department you must have had high clearance and massive skills—you're there for a reason. So Art was a "sir" to us. No doubt about it.

Still, Art looked at us as if *we* were exactly what he was expecting.

As he turned and started out the door, we stared after him. But then he stopped and called back over his shoulder. "Well? Are you coming or aren't ya?"

We got up and followed Art exactly the way we'd come.

No one asked about Mr. Solomon, but one glance at the girls following in the maintenance man's wake told me that we were all wondering the exact same thing.

Well, make that two things: 1.) Where was Mr. Solomon? and 2.) What had happened to Art?

The man walked with a slight limp, his right foot never landing evenly upon the stone floor. His left hand hung against his side at an odd angle, and thick bottle-like glasses must have made the world look very different through his eyes.

But none of that kept him from snapping, "Walters!" when Tina whispered something to Eva, so I'm pretty sure there wasn't anything wrong with his hearing.

We passed ancient wooden doors with locks that looked like they must have required two-ton keys. We climbed higher, past rooms that looked like sets from old monster movies.

When we neared the top, we all walked faster, toward the elevator, anticipating that we were smart enough, seasoned enough, savvy enough to guess what would come next. But one of the golden rules of covert operations is *Always anticipate, never commit*, and that would have been a good time to remember it.

Because Art called, "Ladies!" And the entire class skidded to a stop. We turned to see the man standing in front of one of those enormous doors that, until then, I'd never seen open. He reached inside and flipped on a switch. Light replaced shadow and danced over the stone floor as he took a step on his crooked leg.

"Bex," I whispered as we followed him inside. "Did he seem . . ."

But I didn't finish. Oh, who am I kidding—I *couldn't* finish. Because the room we were stepping into wasn't just an ordinary room. It wasn't a place for an ordinary class.

Rows of clothes lined two long walls. In the center, shelves stood covered with accessories. Mirrors sat in a long row along the back of the room, shelves and drawers, all neatly labeled, sat waiting.

"It's a *closet*," Eva Alvarez said in awe.

"And it's . . . *huge*," Tina Walters replied.

I know normal girls would probably love to find themselves inside a closet two times the size of most suburban houses. But not this closet. This closet could only truly be appreciated by a Gallagher Girl.

We all stepped inside, knowing we were on the verge of a lesson unlike any we'd ever had.

Eva reached out for another switch, and the lights surrounding the mirrors at the back of the room came to life, washing over hats and wigs, glasses and false teeth. Overcoats and umbrellas.

I looked at the man who had brought us there. I turned my gaze from his crippled leg and mangled arm . . . and I knew.

Art stepped to the center of the room and said, "Ladies." He took off his glasses with his left arm, which, for the first time, seemed normal and straight. He kicked off his right shoe, picked it up, and let a small pebble fall into his hand,

and then stood squarely upon his right leg. And then finally he pulled off the gray wig and dropped it onto the low center shelf that ran the length of the room.

Tina Walters gasped. Anna Fetterman stumbled backward. Mr. Solomon was the only one in the room smiling as he swept his arms around the Gallagher Academy closet. "Small changes. Big differences."

He unbuttoned "Art's" shirt and stood in front of us in a white T-shirt (the black trousers, however, he kept on). "Welcome to the science of disguise."

A full minute later, half the class was still staring at Joe Solomon, wondering how old, kinda-pitiful Art could have been the same totally hot guy we had seen every school day for more than a year.

But I was turning, staring at a chameleon's utter fantasy—a place with the sole purpose of making a girl disappear.

And then I saw Bex, and my joy was instantly replaced with unease.

Because she was smiling. And nodding. And whispering, "Plan B?"

Chapter Sixteen

Covert Operations Report

After learning that Operative McHenry was in danger
from a person (or persons) knowing the real identity of
the Gallagher Academy for Exceptional Young Women,
Operatives Morgan, Baxter, and Sutton decided to imple-
ment a shadow operation to oversee Operative McHenry's
security.

It also involved a lot of shadow of the eye variety.

Was it crazy? Yes.

Was it necessary? Maybe.

Was there any way to talk Bex out of it? Only if we
agreed to go with the hog-tying option, so really, it seemed
like our best bet.

We spent all of Friday afternoon researching, planning,
and doing some seriously covert accessorizing, but by

Saturday morning all I could do was walk with Bex and Liz through the halls and fight the combination of nostalgia and nerves that seemed to be growing stronger with every step.

After all, I hadn't been outside the grounds (unofficially) in months; I hadn't opened any of the secret passageways; I hadn't broken any rules. (Okay, I hadn't broken any *big* rules.)

But as I reached for the statue of the Rozell sisters (two identical Gallagher Girls who had posed as double agents—literally—during World War I), I couldn't shake the feeling that I was about to trigger an opening into something much darker and deeper than any secret passageway I'd ever found before.

And that was before I heard Liz cry, "Ew!" and saw her jump back, stumble over Bex's foot, and slam against the wall, skinning her elbow in the process.

The Operatives brought the necessary equipment for a detailed deception-and-disguise operation.

They did not, however, bring the necessary equipment for killing spiders.

Dusty cobwebs hung between the low beams like nature's little surveillance detectors. The biggest spiders I'd ever seen scurried from the light, and I just stood there remembering that there are many, many reasons why a Gallagher Girl should keep in practice. One, you don't want to lose your edge. Two, you never know when you might have to call upon your training. And three, if you go too long without using your secret passages, *other* things tend to take over in your absence.

Even Bex took a big step back. (Because, while Bex is perfectly willing to take on three armed attackers at once, spiders are an entirely different thing.) But Liz was the person I was staring at. After all, there we were, locked inside the safest place in the country, and yet she was already bleeding.

"Hey, Liz, maybe you should stay here. You know . . . set up and run a comms center?"

"That's better if I'm on site," she argued back.

"And cover for us," I added, "if someone starts asking where we are."

"It's Saturday," she reminded me. "In a huge building. That you are notorious for disappearing inside."

"But—" I didn't know what was coming over me, but suddenly I felt like someone should change my nickname from Cammie the Chameleon to Cammie the Corruptor. I was about to break out of my school (again), to do something I wasn't supposed to be doing (again). But that wasn't what worried me as I looked at Liz, who barely weighed a hundred pounds, and then at the secret tunnel that might have been leading us to actual bad guys with actual guns. "Liz, it's just that—"

"Why aren't you telling Bex to stay behind?" Liz shot back, but we all knew the answer: the only way Bex would miss this would be if she were unconscious. And tied up. And locked in a concrete bunker. In Siberia.

Which was a thought that almost made me laugh. Almost. But when I heard Bex say, "Maybe you should sit this one out, Lizzie," I knew my best friend was thinking it too. That once we went forward, there might not be any coming back. In a lot of ways.

Liz is a genius—the kind of genius that puts the rest of us to shame. She no doubt knew the odds. She'd probably calculated the chances of us getting caught, of us getting hurt, and (if it wasn't too traumatic for her to think about) of us getting knocked down a full letter grade on our midterms. But still she turned defiantly and pushed through the cobwebs.

There was no hiding our tracks then—no turning back— so Bex swept her arm across the door, gesturing "after you."

I stepped into the darkness with nothing but my training and my cover and my friends who would follow me to the end of the earth, no matter what was waiting for us on the other side.

Well, it turned out what was waiting for us was a 1987 Dodge minivan.

And Liz had the keys.

"Liz," I said, walking toward her, praying that no one would come driving by and see us. (Partly because we totally weren't supposed to be there. Partly because . . . well . . . it was a *really* ugly minivan.)

But Liz just said, "Get in." Then she stopped. "Who's driving?"

Bex dove for the keys, but given her tendency to forget which side of the road we're supposed to be on, I snatched them out of her grasp.

"Liz," I said again, eyeing the rusty fender, "when you said you could get us a car . . . Liz, where did you get this car?"

"It's a project," she said simply, strapping herself into the backseat.

I pulled at the driver's-side door, and for a second I thought it would fall off its hinges. I looked at the seat. Stuffing was bursting through its fraying seams. The steering wheel was being held together almost entirely by duct tape.

"What kind of project?" I asked, almost afraid of the answer because something told me that pushing that van to Philadelphia wasn't really going to help our mission objectives.

"Oh, give me those," Bex said, grabbing the keys from my hand. She jammed them into the ignition and turned and then . . . nothing.

"Great!" I snapped. "It doesn't even work." But then I felt it. The car was running, but it was almost completely silent, almost completely still.

"New technology," Liz said with a shrug. "Dr. Fibs has been helping me. We've got it up to 250 miles per gallon now," she said, with only the teeniest hint of a gloating smile. "But I think I'll have it doing 325 by Christmas."

And who says Gallagher Girls on the research and operations track never get a chance to save the world?

* * *

We spent the next few hours in silence. Well, if by silence you mean that Liz was rattling on nonstop like she does when she's nervous, and Bex was totally tuning her out like she does when *she's* nervous. And me? I just drove, listening to the rain that started as we crossed the Pennsylvania border. The windshield wipers must not have been as high-tech as the engine because they stuck and stalled, leaving streaks across the glass that caught the light of passing headlights, and by the time we made it to Philadelphia, everything was a blur.

"Right turn," Liz said, navigating our way through narrow cobblestone streets. Buildings older than the Declaration of Independence rose into the rainy sky. Maybe I was expecting the noise of Ohio, the blockades and chaos of the convention, but instead we peered out the grimy windshield onto the slick black streets, and I couldn't help thinking that something felt . . . different.

"Are you sure this is the right place?" I asked. Liz leaned between the two front seats, but before she could act too insulted, we turned and saw a great stone building that covered two city blocks. Massive columns spanned its front entrance, so that it looked more like a Roman temple than a train station. And there, in the center of the facade, was a banner fifty feet long that read WINTERS-MCHENRY: PUTTING AMERICA BACK ON TRACK.

The rain fell harder. Puddles collected on the sidewalks. And beside me, Bex said, "We're here."

Chapter Seventeen

Every mission is a lesson—in school and in life. And before we even reached the doors of the 30th Street station, I learned two very important things.

1. Getting dressed with two other girls in the back of a Dodge minivan should totally be worth extra credit in P&E.
2. Even if they are your best friends, you should never ever trust another operative to pack for you.

"I cannot believe I am wearing this," I muttered as I tugged at the hem of the little black dress Bex had personally smuggled out of Sublevel Two. But it didn't feel like a dress. It felt like . . . torture. Torture with a *very low* back and *very high* shoes.

Stretch limousines were lined up outside the main stairs. Secret Service agents stood guard at every possible exit, but still Bex whispered, "The key to deception and disguise is to break with tendencies and norms."

And right then I knew that having genius friends who are really good at memorizing textbooks can sometimes be a very bad thing, because Bex was right: nothing about that dress was *norm*.

Still, I couldn't help saying, "Then *you* should be wearing it." But Bex just shrugged.

"I'd love to," she said. "And that's the problem."

Here's the thing you need to know about disguise: it's not about being unseen. It's not about being unnoticed. It's about being unrecognized—shedding your own skin. And right then I wasn't worried about the Secret Service or five hundred influential party donors. Right then our only concern was Aunt Abby: fooling her meant leaving our own identities in the van.

I glanced at Liz, whose long blond hair was hidden beneath a dark brown wig. Bex was wearing a wig too, plus glasses and a padded bodysuit that changed the natural silhouette of her athletic frame. We had used every trick in the Gallagher Academy closet, and as we passed the darkened windows of the station, I caught a glimpse of three strangers before realizing that, amazingly, they were us. I didn't even recognize myself under the wig, colored contacts, and fake nose that changed my forgettable face into one that . . . wasn't.

"Okay, gang," I said, "according to blueprints, there's an elevator access panel on the east side of the building. We may get a little dirty, but—"

"I thought we'd just go through the doors," Liz said, flashing three beautifully engraved invitations and some wonderfully authentic fake IDs.

The tickets were $20,000 each. The Secret Service had been vetting the guest list for weeks, so Bex and I stopped beneath a streetlamp and studied Liz.

"Do I even want to know where you got those?" I asked.

Liz seemed to ponder it, and then she said, "No."

And just like that I remembered that Liz was probably the most dangerous one of us all.

Stepping inside the station was like stepping inside another world. Beautiful carvings covered a ceiling that was at least fifty feet tall. A string quartet played from the second-story balcony, their music echoing off the stone floors, while five hundred men and women ate and drank and talked about the road to the White House.

I didn't want to think about the kind of favors someone had had to call in to close down the entire station for the night (and come to think of it, an actual act of Congress might have been involved), so I just stood at the top of the steps with my best friends and a great statue of the angel Michael, who held a fallen soldier in his arms, his wings poised to take flight. Somehow, it felt like all four of us were on the lookout for Macey.

"Any sign?" I asked twenty minutes later as I walked through the crowd.

"Negative," Bex replied.

"Wow, did you guys know the Pennsylvania train system dates back to—"

"Liz!" Bex and I snapped in unison.

"It's Bookworm," Liz corrected, and I couldn't really complain.

"Bookworm, what did the official agenda say again?" I asked, needing to hear it.

"It said Macey will be making one public appearance today. She'll be arriving at seven thirty via the Back on Track Express—whatever that is."

"What time is it?" I said.

"You know what time it is," Bex reminded me, but I was hoping I was wrong, because the candidates and their families were . . . late.

Late meant mistakes.

Mistakes meant problems.

And problems . . . well, I really didn't want to think about what those meant.

Mr. Solomon's warning kept coming back to me as I surveyed the crowd, remembering that the bad guys could be anyone, that they could be anywhere—that they knew who we were. And they just had to get lucky . . . once.

Maybe it was my spy training; maybe it was a crazy, hyperactive imagination, but it seemed like everywhere I looked, people seemed suspicious.

There was a man with a red bow tie who bumped into me not once, not twice, but three times and was a little . . . handsy. My first instinct was to call out for Macey on the comms to see if he was flirting, but then I remembered that the one Gallagher Girl who was certain to have an answer to that question was the one Gallagher Girl I couldn't ask.

"Chameleon," Bex's voice rang in my ear. "Cammie, are you—"

"I'm here," I said.

"What's wrong?" her accent was heavy again.

"Nothing. I mean—" I was spinning, being about as uncovert as I could possibly be, but something was . . . wrong.

"Eyes," I said, citing an operative's ultimate resource—her instincts. "I feel eyes. Someone's . . . watching."

"Yeah," Bex said, her voice thick with a resounding *duh*. "You look hot."

Well, that explained one thing, because covert I'm good at. Invisible I'm good at. Hot I am totally *not* good at.

I pushed through the crowds again, knowing that it was getting later and later, and I couldn't help worrying more and more. Flashes of Boston went through my mind. I closed my eyes and shuddered, saw an almost identical crowd, felt that almost identical feeling.

"Bookworm, Duchess," I started, but then I stopped because I didn't have a clue how that sentence was supposed to end.

"Any sign of them?" I asked instead.

"No buses," Liz told me from her vantage point by the window.

"No sign at the east entrance. Wait," Bex said, stopping short.

The feeling of the crowd was changing. An energy so

palpable was coursing through the old historic station that I looked out the massive windows at the cloudy sky, half expecting lightning.

"Oh my gosh," Liz exclaimed, echoing Bex's surprise.

"What?" I said out loud, not caring if anyone noticed. I spun, looking at the station's main entrance, but then I felt the crowd shift behind me. I turned slowly and realized there was no bus. There was no convoy.

Instead, a long, ancient-looking train with old-fashioned red, white, and blue bunting hanging from the caboose was slowly moving into the station.

In the next instant it didn't matter how great our comms units were, because the cry that came up from five hundred rabid voters was enough to drown out even the sound of my best friends' voices in my ear.

Governor Winters and Macey's dad stepped out onto the stage behind the caboose, and then their wives. Macey and Preston were one step behind them.

I waited for the fear in my stomach to subside. I told myself I was crazy. After all, Macey was smiling. She was waving. She was the perfect operative with the perfect cover. Aunt Abby was beside her. She was fine.

For a second a wave of relief like nothing I'd ever known swept over me. But then the crowd shifted, and for a split second my gaze fell on a man.

A man with crazy white hair and wild eyebrows.

A man I had seen before.

In Boston.

Chapter eighteen

It didn't mean it was something. Odds were, it was probably nothing. After all, there were probably a lot of people who went to political conventions *and* political rallies. And the Secret Service was there—the Secret Service was *good*.

Still, I didn't know what was scarier, that I'd seen a man in the crowd who I'd literally bumped into on the very day my roommate had been attacked, or that—just that quickly—the familiar face had vanished.

"Duchess!" I practically shouted, but the crowd was too loud, the race too close, and the people who wanted the Winters-McHenry ticket to win on Election Day were too fired up as I called through our comms units for my friends. "Duchess, there was a guy . . . in a suit . . ." I climbed the main staircase to better scan the platform, and that's where I realized that I'd just described half of the clapping crowd. "A dark suit," I added. "Crazy-looking white hair.

Wild eyebrows. Mustache," I rattled off identifying charac-
teristics as quickly as I could think of them.

The Operative realized that incredibly high heels made
it very hard to pursue people quickly across very slick
floors!

The band played. People drank. And where the train
stood at the end of the platform, I saw the face again. I recognized something in the way he moved, and my mind
flashed back to the hotel lobby in Boston while the Texas
delegation sang.

And then I glanced at the train and saw Aunt Abby
standing in the wings, ten feet from Macey and exactly
where she was supposed to be. And the white-haired man
moved closer.

I didn't know how to describe him, and that was maybe
the most notable thing of all. He was just moving through
the crowd as if there were someplace else he had to be. Call
me crazy, but I couldn't shake the feeling that no one pays
$20,000 to leave in the middle of the main event.

I hurried through the crowd as quickly as I dared without A) falling down, and B) attracting attention. And I was
doing pretty well at both, until a waiter picked that moment
to lose his grip on a tray of champagne. As the glasses fell, I
sidestepped and spun.

And ran right in to Preston Winters.

"Oh, I'm so sorry!" he exclaimed, gripping me by the

shoulders as if I were about to fall down. (Which I wasn't, but he probably didn't need to know that I've had entire sections of Protection and Enforcement class dedicated to helping an operative keep her balance.) "Are you okay? Can I get you some . . . punch . . . or something?"

"I'm fine, thank you, though," I said as I ran through the mental checklist of things that were going wrong at that moment, forgetting the most troublesome thing of all.

"Have we met before?" Preston asked, looking at me in a way that said that, despite the long black wig and tight black dress, there was something way too familiar about me.

"No, I don't believe we have," I said in my best Southern accent. I tried to pull away. The man was easing down the length of the train and into the stone tunnel from which it had emerged, and I just stood there thinking about my options.

The Operative regretted not packing Dr. Fibs's new Band-Aid-style Napotine patches. She also regretted not packing some regular Band-Aids, because her shoes really did hurt her feet.

Preston's father stood on a makeshift stage behind the caboose of the old-fashioned train—a physical homage to better times—and told the crowd, "We're going to get America *back on track*!" The crowd cheered, but I was too busy listening to two voices. One belonged to the boy in front of me, who was asking, "I know, you were at the Atlanta rally, weren't you?" The other buzzed in my ear as

Bex cried, "You guys are *never* going to believe who's here! Eyes," she said again. "I have eyes on—"

But then there was nothing but static as my roommate's voice faded away. My first thought was to bring my hand to my ear and scream like a total amateur, but I didn't.

"Now, I just know we've met before," Preston went on, oblivious to the panic I was feeling. "Come on. Help me out." I could have lied. I could have fought. But desperate times call for desperate measures, so I took a chance and called upon a Gallagher Girl's weapon of last resort. I flirted.

"I'm sorry," I said, batting my false eyelashes. "I just get a little tongue-tied anytime I'm around such a handsome man."

"Um . . ." Preston swallowed hard. "Handsome?" Instantly, I felt the tables turn.

"Yes," I replied, reaching to grip his bicep. "I swear, you are even stronger than you look on TV."

He swallowed again and somehow managed to mutter, "You know I lift . . . *things.*"

"Oh, I can tell." In my ear, Bex's voice was drowning in static, but my mission at that moment was to get away from Preston Winters without him realizing that the girl in the black dress was also the girl on the roof. "You know, this is my favorite of your suits. I also like the navy pinstripe, of course, but you were wearing that one in Boston, weren't you? So now *this* is my favorite. . . ." I started to chatter on about which of Preston's ties went better with his eyes, but before I could say a word, Preston was already pointing to his parents across the room.

"Wait. Oh, you know, I think they need me for . . . stuff."

"Oh, but—" I said as he started to walk away.

"Thank you for your vote," he called, turning back.

But I was already gone.

"Duchess," I tried as I inched closer to the train tunnel. "Duchess," I tried again, with one glance back at the party, at Macey and Aunt Abby, and I knew I had two choices. One, I could wave down my aunt, which would result in reinforcements and the possibility that she would tell my mother what I was doing. Or two, I could follow a person of interest in a kidnapping attempt into a dark tunnel, without backup, without help.

So I did the second one because, at the time, it was the least scary of my options.

As I stepped inside the dim space, the sound of the crowd faded behind me while, in my ear, my comms unit began to crack and buzz.

I strolled down the darkened tunnel, my (totally uncomfortable) shoes as quiet as a whisper against the cold concrete. But that was before a hand clasped over my mouth, an arm gripped me tightly around my waist, and someone pulled me out of my shoes.

"Hey, Chameleon, how's it going?" Bex's voice sounded strong in my ear.

My first thought was to struggle against the arms that were holding me. My second was, Hey, how can Bex be talking in my ear if my comms unit is out?

But then the arms released me and I spun to face my best friend. "What are you doing in here?" I asked.

She smiled. "Guess who else made the drive up from Roseville?" she asked, her eyes twinkling.

"Bex, it's Saturday. I'd really rather not take a quiz if I can help it."

Then she gripped my shoulders and turned me around. "*Look.*"

The first time I ever saw Joe Solomon, he was strolling into the Grand Hall during the welcome-back dinner of my sophmore year. None of us knew where he'd come from or why he was there. Standing in the shadows, it wasn't hard to remember how that had felt.

"He's hot in a tuxedo," Bex said, and I started to snap because . . . well . . . it kind of went without saying, and also we had other things to worry about. Some seriously important other things. Because just then Mr. Solomon wasn't alone anymore.

"Ooh, he has a hot tuxedoed friend," Bex teased. But I knew better—I'd seen that man and his wild white hair and crazy eyebrows before. I'd *seen* him. In Boston.

The two men spoke for a moment, then Mr. Solomon turned and started to walk away, varying his pace in order to hear the footsteps of anyone who might be following in the dark tunnel, a textbook countersurveillance procedure if ever there was one. Bex winked at me, more than up for the challenge, then slipped into the tunnel a safe distance behind our teacher. But I just kept staring at the guy left in Joe Solomon's wake.

Someone Mr. Solomon knew.

Someone Mr. Solomon seemed to respect.

Someone who had a knack for being where Macey—and I—happened to be.

Maybe it was some inherent hotness that Bex had seen and I'd missed. Maybe it was the way the man with the white hair had straightened in the dark tunnel and moved with grace that didn't belong with the rest of his body. But for some reason, I thought back to the way Mr. Solomon had stood in "Art's" uniform and told us how the art of deception and disguise isn't complex—it's simple: just give the eyes something new to look at so that the mind doesn't truly *see*.

My mind flew from Boston and back again, the déjà vu growing stronger, the pieces of a puzzle falling into place. I closed my eyes and saw eyes and not eyebrows, a mouth and not a mustache. I stripped away the cover piece by piece until I stood in the dark, finally seeing.

"Zach."

I have to admit that at that moment I had seriously mixed feelings about the situation. I had seen Zach! Sure, he was wearing a disguise. Sure, all boys (much less Blackthorne Boys) are probably experts at the art of deception!

But that didn't change the fact that I'd thought I'd seen him a dozen times before actually coming face-to-face with him in Ohio. And at that moment, I knew better. I breathed, realizing that, on the one hand, I hadn't had Zach on the brain in Boston. My mind hadn't been playing tricks on me. I wasn't boy—or any kind of—crazy.

On the other hand, I'd had him on my tail, and as a spy I didn't know which was worse.

The Secret Service was standing guard at the ends of the tunnel, but a small service hatch was open, a cart loaded with trays of food and crates of beverages was waiting to be wheeled on board. Zach walked slowly toward it, and then in a flash he vanished.

For a second I had to blink, but there wasn't a doubt in my mind where he'd gone. The only thing left to wonder . . . was why.

I could see Bex nearing the end of the tunnel, still keeping her distance from Mr. Solomon. As soon as she left the tunnel and got back reception on her comms unit, she would tell Liz that she had eyes on our teacher. In the distance, the string quartet was playing the same song we'd heard in Ohio, following the same speeches. Steam gushed from the train beside me. I heard the metallic groan of a machine that wouldn't be held back for long.

And I did the only thing I could.

I got on board.

Chapter nineteen

I learned a lot that day. Like never let Bex pick the snacks during road trip stops. Always bring a spare pair of shoes. And a half hour later, I knew to add one more thing to the list:

Never, ever volunteer to do surveillance on a moving train.

Especially if the train is also occupied by your aunt, one of your best friends (who doesn't exactly know you're there), and thirty-seven members of the United States Secret Service!

The train was seventeen cars of narrow aisle and armed guards, of tight compartments and people high on polling numbers and caffeine. So I lowered my head and squeezed down the aisle and tried not to forget that, when faced with being somewhere you're not supposed to be, rule number one is simple: be someone else.

I picked up the nearest clipboard and moved purposefully down the crowded aisle. The engines squeaked, coming to life. The compartments buzzed. And I kept moving, smiling, acting like I was thrilled to be a part of history.

Zach could have been anywhere, and judging from his disguise-and-deception abilities so far, he could have been *anyone*. So I kept pushing my way down the corridor, rocking with the moving train, until one of the interns called to me. "Hey, where are you going?"

"New speech for Peacock," I said, flashing the clipboard and rolling my eyes.

"Oooh," one of the guys said, making a sympathetic face. "Compartment fourteen," he said, pointing to the next car. "Have fun," he mocked, and I knew Macey's cover was still firmly in place as I opened the door to the connecting car.

I eased down the crowded aisle, not knowing what I'd find. But just then I knew I might have made the biggest mistake of my life. Behind me, I heard a very distinct voice coming through the crowd, saying, "Peacock is moving."

I was away from school. And in a disguise. And wearing a very little black dress while my favorite (and only) aunt was coming up behind me!

A door stood on my left, number fourteen. I pressed my ear against it but heard nothing. I tried the handle. Locked. Of course.

"Yes," Abby's voice was saying, growing closer.

I was desperate. I knocked. "Ms. McHenry, are you in there? May I have a word?" I asked, still clinging to my cover.

"Absolutely," Abby said behind me. "A four-hundred-foot perimeter should be more than ample."

I was *really* desperate. I pulled a bobby pin out of my hair. And tried the lock.

I felt the lock turn just as Abby pushed free of the crowd, and in the next second I was surrounded by darkness.

I felt someone grab for me, but I dodged it.

A hand grabbed my hair—or what it thought was my hair—and pulled the wig free. Abby's voice was louder now—right outside—and inside the tiny compartment everything went still.

There was a faint yellow glow in a small crack beneath the door, and in the light I saw Zach look from the wig and then to me and then back again.

"You aren't supposed to be here, Gallagher Girl." It wasn't playful. It wasn't fun. He wasn't smiling or flirting. He was . . .

Mad.

Mad like I'd never seen him. Mad like I didn't even know he could be. I've always known that Zach was strong (a girl doesn't spar with a guy in P&E for a semester and not figure that out), but right then he was like stone.

The first thing that hit me was the shock. The second . . . was the anger.

"You're telling *me* that *I* shouldn't be here?" I snapped. Sure, my aunt and half the United States Secret Service were probably right outside the door at that moment, and yet I couldn't stop myself.

"It's dangerous," he said.

"In case you haven't noticed, I can take care of myself."

Unfortunately, the train picked that moment to lurch,

and despite the best protection-and-enforcement training in the world, I found myself stumbling, falling into Zach's outstretched arms.

I started to pull away, but he held me.

"Shhh," he said as the voices in the hall outside faded for a second.

And then the scariest thing of all happened: Zach looked like he wanted to kiss me. . . .

But he didn't.

He was the same boy who had dipped me movie-style in front of my whole school in the middle of finals week, and yet there we were, crammed together in the dark of a moving train, adrenaline and drizzle hanging all around us, and he didn't make a single move.

"Nice disguise," he told me, smiling at last.

"You too," I said. I thought about that moment—what it meant, how long I wanted it to last, and what I was willing to give up to find the truth. So that's why I added, "It looked even better in Boston."

There are moments in a spy's life when time speeds up, and then there are seconds that last a lifetime. And this . . . this was one of those instances that seemed to go on for years. In the narrow space, with Zach's arms still wrapped around me and voices still echoing outside, I watched his expression shift from confusion to shock to the look of someone desperate for a plan.

"Yeah, I—"

Someone was knocking. My eyes were wide as they stared into his.

"Here," he said, gesturing to the collapsible overhead sleeping bunks that, before that moment, I'd only ever seen in old movies.

More knocking.

Outside, someone yelled, "Who's got a key for this?"

But by the time the door burst open, Zach and I were nowhere to be seen.

(Note to self: don't become a spy if you're even a little bit claustrophobic.)

"What's going on, Zach?" I whispered through the pitch blackness of the little collapsible bunk. That we had collapsed. With ourselves locked inside.

His arm was around my waist. His breath was warm on the back of my neck. Sure, I could hear Aunt Abby in the tiny compartment saying, "Macey, I don't want to argue about this anymore. Just wait in here," but I didn't really care.

"You were in Boston, Zach."

"Shhh," he whispered, pulling me closer with a jerk around my middle.

Outside our tiny bunk I heard more voices coming from compartment fourteen. I would have known Macey's speech pattern anywhere. But the other voice was familiar too, and yet I couldn't quite . . .

"You know," the deeper of the two voices said, "I've been told this is my best suit."

Preston!

I heard more talking and music, but all of that seemed a

million miles away as I lay there, my mind racing faster than the train.

"*That's* how you knew about the laundry chute," I hissed, another piece of the puzzle falling into place. "Why were you there, Zach?" I whispered, growing desperate.

"Not now." His voice was soft but strong.

"And don't say it was because we were in danger, because at the time we *weren't* in any danger."

"You want to take a nap or something?" he whispered.

"Yeah, and while we're on the subject, why are you *here?*"

"I could ask the same thing of you, Gallagher Girl, except we should be *shutting up* now."

Which was a very good idea because the voices outside had stopped. Macey and Preston weren't talking anymore, but the spy (not to mention the girl) in me knew somehow that they were still out there. Because there were sounds. Sounds I recognized. Sounds I really didn't want to think too much about. Because I think they were the sounds of kissing.

And I was currently smashed up against a boy that I had kissed!

And at that moment kissing needed to be the furthest thing from my mind!

"What were you and Mr. Solomon talking about?" I said, because, frankly, I really needed to say something!

But Zach must have been immune to the kissing sounds. Or kissing thoughts, because he snapped, "You don't get it, do you?" He twisted me somehow so that our faces were inches away from each other in the black. "This is dangerous,

Cammie," he said, not Gallagher Girl. "This is—"

"Yeah. I kinda figured that out the day I woke up with a concussion."

"Don't make light of this."

"What about 'concussion' is synonymous with 'making light'?"

"You shouldn't be here," he said again slowly, like I wasn't bright enough to keep up.

"*You're* here," I snapped back.

"Listen, this is no place for . . ."

"A girl?"

The train may have been swarming with armed guards . . . My roommate and the potential future first son of the United States may have been making out a few feet away . . . The world as I knew it may have been on the verge of being over if Zach and I had gotten caught. . . .

But I. Didn't. Care.

"A student?" I tried again. "What, Zach? Tell me what you are that I'm not."

And then my eyes must have adjusted to the black, because I swear I could see him—really, truly see him—as the cockiest boy I'd ever known looked at me and whispered, "I'm someone who doesn't have anything to lose."

Everything else went away then—the noise from outside, the rocking of the car, the pressure, and the fatigue. I don't know what would have happened next. Maybe I would have cried. Maybe I would have given in. Or maybe I would have demanded more answers to the questions I barely dared to ask.

But we'll never know.

Because just as Zach touched my face, the world fell out from underneath us. Gravity took hold. One moment I was lying in the arms of one of the most complex (and gorgeous) boy spies ever, and the next I was landing like a ton of bricks on the hard, cold floor of a moving train while one of my best friends stared down at me. And the boy on top of me. And said, "Well, *this* wasn't on my agenda."

At least Preston was gone—or at least I thought Preston was gone. I couldn't be too sure because it was taking me a second to get my bearings.

"Ms. McHenry!" a male voice shouted from the other side of the door. "Secret Service! Is everything okay?"

I stared up at Macey. Zach was splayed on top of me, one of his legs tangled with Macey's backpack. A tray of food had fallen with us and was now splattered all over the floor.

Macey looked at us, the most unusual look on her face, as if she knew that, with a single word she could bring that door—and our entire world—crashing down. She smiled, savoring the moment before she slowly said, "Everything's fine. I just knocked over a tray."

"Shall we send a porter to—"

"No!" Macey snapped. "I want to be alone, or is that too hard to understand?"

I heard retreating footsteps.

Macey dropped to the bench across from us while Zach and I tried to right ourselves.

"Hi, Zach," she said, her right leg swinging as she sat with it crossed over her left.

"Hey, Macey," he said, as if he fell out of ceilings and into the private chambers of the most highly protected girl in the country every day. "Sorry to drop in," he said with a look that told me he thought he was entirely too clever, "but Cammie just had to be alone with me. You know how she gets."

I smacked his arm.

He flinched. "You know, you're going to hurt me one of these days, and then you're going to feel really bad about it."

"Yeah," I started, "well, maybe if you would be honest with me for one—"

"Um, just so you know," Macey said, cutting me off as she leaned back, enjoying the show, "Abby will be back in approximately two minutes, so you lovebirds might want to make this quick."

I totally expected the boy in front of me to recoil at the word "lovebirds." But he didn't. Instead he grabbed the bag he'd been carrying and turned to Macey. "Thanks." He placed his knee on the bench and leaned toward the dark window, staring into the black as he said, "This is my stop anyway."

Well, from what I could tell, the train wasn't stopping. It wasn't even slowing down.

"Hey, McHenry, you mind?" He gestured to the door then stepped back as Macey opened it and checked the aisle.

"Oh, officer," she called to the sentry stationed in the hall outside. "Can I see your gun?"

As the man turned his back on us, Zach dashed out into the hall and to the door at the end of the car. I started to follow, but he stopped suddenly and turned to me. "Hey, Gallagher Girl," he said, looking at me more deeply than he ever had, "promise me something."

The train was faster now. Night streamed through the windows. And Zach stepped even closer.

"Be"—he reached up and gently touched the place where my bruise had been as if it were still fresh and swollen—"careful."

And then Zach stepped to the end of the car and slid open the door. The noise was overpowering for an instant. We were going over a great ravine, nothingness streaming on both sides as Zach spread his arms out wide. He looked back at me for one fleeting second.

And jumped into the night.

"So . . ." the voice behind me was strong and even. I turned to see a very sorry-looking Macey and a very impressed-looking Aunt Abby staring at me and the fading parachute that was Zach. "I take it that's the man in your life."

Chapter Twenty

When an operative is compromised mid-mission, there are a lot of things that have to be said. And done. For example, it's great if you have a legend or two you can whip out to distract the catcher from the catchee's actual intentions. Also, misdirection is always useful, so you can place blame on anyone but yourself. Or you can retreat.

But we were on a moving train.

And I didn't have a parachute.

And Aunt Abby was staring right at me.

I expected her to smile like she'd done when she pulled me out from under her bed, but instead she glared at me with a look that was equal parts fury and fear, as Macey and I darted back into compartment fourteen.

"Sit," my aunt commanded, and we each sat on the lower berth while my aunt began to pace. "Do you know what you've done?" she asked, but it wasn't really a question. "Do you know what could have happened tonight?"

Her voice shook. I feared for a second that the Secret Service might come through the door again, but the train was loud and the rain was hard and we kept barreling through the night. I glanced around the small space. It was no use. I, Cammie the Chameleon, had absolutely no place to hide.

"Do you have any idea how dangerous this all is? If the Secret Service caught you . . . If a member of the media caught a glimpse of what you can do . . . If there are two girls in the school—in the world—who should know better than to take chances like this, it should be the two of you!"

"I thought rules were made to be broken," I said, confused at first but growing angry. "I thought being a spy was rules-optional," I said, throwing her own words back at her.

"Being a spy means you never have the luxury of being careless!" The train rocked and the night grew darker as my aunt leaned closer and said, "Trust me, Cameron. That is one lesson you don't want to learn the hard way."

Maybe it was the sound of the rain, or the look in her eyes, but I couldn't stop thinking about the way she'd changed in my mother's office, morphed from the Abby I knew into a woman I had never seen before. And just that quickly I realized the smiling, laughing, dancing woman who had walked into my life after four and a half years was just another cover—a Gallagher Girl pretending to be something that she's not.

"Where were you, Aunt Abby?" I heard myself ask. "Dad died, and you weren't there," I said, remembering a time in my life that I'd done everything to forget. I heard my voice crack, felt my eyes blur. I told myself it was the steady rocking of the train that made me feel unsteady, but I knew better as I shouted, "He died and you didn't even come to the funeral. You didn't call. You didn't visit. Dad died, and ever since then *you've* been a ghost."

Abby turned her back to me. She started for the door, but those words had been alive in me for years, the doubts and questions stacked end to end, and I couldn't stop them if I'd tried.

"We needed you!" I thought about my mother, who still cried when she thought no one could see her, and before I even realized it, I was crying too. "Why weren't you there when we needed you?"

"Haven't you learned yet, Cam?" Abby's voice was softer now, as if she were being dragged back into a dream. "There are some things you don't want to know."

I could feel the train—or maybe just the world—slowing down as she stepped toward the door and whispered, "Stay away from that boy, Cammie." It wasn't an order this time, it was a plea.

"Zach?" Macey asked, as if there could possibly be anyone else. "He's from Blackthorne. We know him."

Then Abby looked at me. For the first time, it seemed like she wanted to smile, but there was no joy in her expression as she asked, "Do you?"

I love the Gallagher Academy at night. There's beauty in the shadows—the only time when the outside really reflects what's going on inside. Nothing is truly black or white. The whole world in shades of gray.

And that night was no different.

"What does *that* mean?" Liz asked, and Bex paced, but I just stood at the little diamond-shaped window in our attic suite, looking out at the dark grounds, letting the story I'd just told wash over me.

"Wait, you mean Zach got to jump out of a moving train?" Bex asked, not even trying to hide the envy in her voice.

I looked at Macey, who shrugged.

"I still can't believe you left the mansion like that," she said, examining my short skirt and tall shoes.

I tried to smile. "Originally, there was also a wig."

I expected her to laugh. I wanted her to roll her eyes or say something about the world of synthetic hair and people fashion-deprived enough to actually utilize it. I wanted it to be funny. But it wasn't.

"So Abby was really . . ." Liz started, then lowered her voice, *"mad?"*

I nodded. The word didn't do it justice, but at the moment, it was the only one I had.

"You're not going to get into trouble, Cam," Bex argued. "Abby's cool."

But she hadn't seen the change in Abby on the train. She hadn't heard the tremor in my aunt's voice or seen the look in her eyes as she strolled through the Hall of History and into my mother's office and closed the door, leaving Macey and me to make our way upstairs alone.

"What?" Bex asked, proving that she knew me maybe better than I knew myself.

"He . . ." I struggled with what I wanted to say, what I wanted to believe. "He didn't kiss me."

Yes, I'd just been severely reprimanded by a member of the United States Secret Service. And yes, I'd been caught sneaking out and violating about a dozen school rules. And yes, my elbow was totally swollen from where Zach and I had landed on the floor of Macey's compartment.

And yet that was the thing that worried me most.

"He didn't flirt," I said finally. "He didn't tease me . . . I mean, once I figured out I'd seen him in Boston—"

"Wait," Bex said, moving closer, completely ignoring the big pile of junk food that she and Liz had smuggled back into the school after their road trip home. There was something new in her eyes as she said, "Zach was in Boston?"

"I kept *thinking* I saw him there," I said again, calmer now. "But I thought that I was . . . you know . . ."

Bex and Liz looked at each other as if they totally didn't know.

"She thought she was only seeing him because she *wanted* to see him," Macey explained.

"Ooooh," Bex and Liz sighed together.

"It's a by-product of very dramatic kissing," Macey went on like a doctor identifying a common side effect. "Go on."

"So I didn't think anything about it. But today I saw him again. And he was in the same disguise, and I knew it was him in Boston." I looked down at the pile of candy wrappers and half-eaten bags of chips and thought about how, a year ago, we'd huddled together in that very room, going through Josh's trash, but there was a lot about boys and their dirty little secrets that we still had to learn.

"So he followed you before?" Liz asked. "So what? He's probably just doing what *we're* doing—tracking Macey."

And then she stopped. And realized.

"In Boston, there was no reason to track Macey," I said, just because I needed to say the words out loud. I looked back at the grounds that seemed darker than usual. And colder. Somehow when I wasn't looking, fall had fallen, and I shivered a little, still chilled from the rain.

"Maybe he knew what was going to happen," Macey said.

"Or maybe he was one of the people doing it," Bex said, the old skepticism coming back to her voice.

"Or"—Liz's eyes were the only ones shining as she said—"he wanted to be near Cammie!"

Macey shrugged as if to say that our little blond friend had a point.

Whatever the case, that didn't change the fact that a very cute, very mysterious spy boy was either out to save us, or kidnap us, or date us.

And I wasn't sure which one we were best equipped to handle.

I don't know about normal girls, but for spy girls, there are few things as scary as a closed door, a locked room, and a whispered conversation you can't quite hear. Well, the next day my life was full of all three.

The Hall of History remained dark. My mother's office doors remained closed (and, unfortunately, soundproof). I thought about the passageway that led behind the room, but then I shook the notion from my head. I didn't know what my aunt had told her. I didn't know what kind of trouble I was in.

All around me girls worried about tests and projects. People opened letters from home and continued the debate about whether or not Mr. Smith's new face made him as hot as Mr. Solomon. But I couldn't help but think about how the world is just a web of secrets. I kept wondering if there was any way to break free.

That Sunday night I walked toward my mother's office, thinking about Abby and Zach, Philadelphia and Boston— all the questions no one ever answered, but as I stepped foot inside the Hall of History, I found myself looking at Gilly's sword.

I heard myself whisper, "Someone knows."

As I knocked on the door to my mother's office, I knew it wasn't going to be an ordinary Sunday night supper. . . .

Because Macey was already there.

I looked from my mother, to my roommate, and finally to my aunt. I expected yelling. But when my mother whispered, "Cammie," it was worse. Way worse. The door closed behind me, and I saw Mr. Solomon standing there. I didn't know what to expect anymore.

"Mom, I—"

"I was told that Liz and Bex were out testing a prototype of a new piece of equipment for Dr. Fibs during your little . . . *mission* last night?" Mom asked.

Her eyes seemed to be warning me not to argue. "Yes," I quickly answered.

"Very well."

For a second I thought that might be all of it, but of course the lecture wasn't over. "Cameron, I trusted you to believe me when I said that Macey's safety was no longer your concern."

"Yes, ma'am."

"I trusted you to know that security protocol is not something that should be interfered with on a whim."

"Yes, ma'am."

"I trusted you, Cammie." My mother's voice was softer then, so that was the hardest part to hear.

"I received a call from Bex's mother last night," Mom continued, and I braced for the wrath of two spy moms scorned. "The Baxters would like for you to spend winter break in London—"

"Really?" I asked in surprise.

"And if I hear," Mom spoke over me. "If I see . . . If I even *suspect* that you have been out of these grounds again without permission, then that will not happen. Am I making myself clear?"

"Yes," I said, feeling the weight of the situation settling down on me.

"The latest polls have the race neck and neck," my mother said. She was too calm. Too easy. "It's understandable then that Macey's parents are going to want her with them as much of that time as—"

"No!"

"—possible," Mom went on as if I hadn't said a word.

I glanced at Macey. She'd been quiet all day, but standing in my mother's office, her silence seemed infinitely louder.

"That will, of course," Mom said slowly, "be something we will not allow."

I'd already opened my mouth to protest when I heard her and stopped short.

"You mean," Macey was saying beside me, "you mean I won't have to . . . go?"

"No," Mr. Solomon said. "Frankly, Ms. McHenry, the risk is too high. We want you at home where you belong."

I've lived with Macey for a long time, but one thing every spy learns eventually is that you never know everything, and I'd never seen Macey look like she looked then. I thought about the girl who had crawled out of the limo, and the girl she had become before this crazy election started changing her back. It was as if the word "home" was a code—a signal—and that alone told her she was safe and she could lower her guard.

"Assuming that's okay with you?" my mother asked, and Macey nodded.

Mr. Solomon stepped away from the door, so like any good operatives (not to mention teenage girls in trouble), we bolted for it.

"Oh, Cammie," Mom called for me, and I stopped while Macey moved on ahead. Mr. Solomon and Aunt Abby followed my roommate outside and closed the door as my mother stepped closer. "Don't worry about Macey, Cam." But it wasn't a soothing phrase. It was an order. "The Secret Service is very good at what they do. For all our differences, my sister is very, very good at what she does. I do not want you worrying about Macey."

"Okay."

"I mean it."

"So do I," I said. And in that moment, I really did.

"I knew you were in the compartment." Macey's voice sliced through the Hall of History. Down in the Grand Hall, girls were eating, people were gossiping, but Macey just sat on the top step looking into the foyer as if she didn't have the strength to stand.

"I didn't hear you or anything," she went on as I walked closer. "It was just a . . . feeling." Then she looked at me. "You know?"

"Yeah," I said, and I did.

"The top sleeping compartment was hanging too low, and the magazine on the bench had shifted, and I just . . . knew."

Then she looked at me. "I'm good at this, right?"

"Yeah. You are."

"When your mom called me in, I thought . . . I thought she was gonna kick me out." She shrugged a little. "Usually that's when I get kicked out."

I've seen Macey without makeup and in her fat jeans. I've heard what she says in her sleep and seen the way her lips move when she's reading and the words just won't sink in. I know Macey McHenry, but that night, sitting on that staircase, I realized I'd never know what it's like to *be* her.

The McHenrys have five houses, but this is Macey's only home. She's the most famous daughter in America, but Liz and Bex and I are her only family.

"No one's gonna kick you out, Macey." I tried to laugh. "You know too much. By now we'd have to kill you."

It took forty-seven seconds, but eventually Macey smiled. Eventually she laughed.

"So, Preston?" I said, because, honestly, I was sort of about to explode. And . . . okay . . . so it had taken me practically twenty-four hours to mention it, but I'd had other things on my mind. Like my sanity, my future, and whether or not Zach's sudden disinterest in kissing had anything to do with the fact that my hair tends to get frizzy when it's raining. But that didn't stop me from leaning closer and whispering, "Did I or did I not hear you kissing Preston?"

"There are people I could hire to kill you and make it look like an accident."

I gripped the banister and propelled myself up a couple of steps. "He's not so bad."

"Seriously. There wouldn't even be an inquest." Macey took a step then added, "Besides, do I have to tell you that secret boyfriends are the hottest?"

In spite of everything, I smiled. "Point taken."

Chapter twenty-one

I still remember the day—the moment—when I found my very first secret passage. I had been at school three days. My mom had just started her job. My dad had just died. And I'd just arrived at the school I'd heard about my entire life (or, well, the parts of my life that came after the part where I figured out that my mom and dad had more *covert* reasons for missing my kindergarten graduation).

I was wandering the hallways, wondering about this building that was bigger and older and more beautiful than anything I'd ever seen. Wondering how long it would take for me to realize that my mom would never go away again and my dad would never come back.

Wondering if I really belonged at the Gallagher Academy and if I was truly worthy to carry both the Morgan *and* Cameron family names.

But then I stopped in the hallway by the library.

A window was open. The school still had the stale

feeling of a building that had been underoccupied for a long time, and I watched as a breeze blew through the windows and pushed some dust along the stone-tiled floor, rolling dirt through the cracks like water in a river. But at one point, instead of rolling along, it dropped out of sight as if there were a waterfall in the grout that could barely be seen by the naked eye, disappearing beneath a wall of solid stone.

I pushed and pulled for five minutes before the wall slid open, and I found my first way of disappearing in plain sight.

Three days before I'd found it. Three days I'd been at this place I loved. Three days . . .

And already I was looking for ways out.

And that was before I was forbidden to leave.

———

PROS AND CONS OF BEING GROUNDED INSIDE THE MOST AWESOME GROUNDS IN THE WORLD:

PRO: It's a lot easier to protect your roommate from the people who want to kidnap her if she spends most of her time in your room.

CON: When Mr. Mosckowitz asks you to help him proof his paper for the Excellence in European Encryption seminar on Friday night, you can't say "Sorry, I'm going to be out of town."

PRO: Staying out of secret, ancient tunnels means you don't get nearly as many questionable stains on your white blouse.

CON: When your roommate tests a landmark discovery in clean-fuel technology (that happens to reside inside a Dodge minivan), you don't get to ride shotgun.

PRO: You don't have to worry about running into the boy who may or may not have been stalking you.

CON: You don't get to run into the boy who may or may not have been protecting you. (Even though you don't really need protecting, it totally is the thought that counts.)

PRO: You have plenty of time to think.

CON: You don't always like what you're thinking about.

Zach hadn't tried to kiss me.

Of course, there *are* bigger mysteries in the world, and I'm sure the CIA would have classified that information as a low-level concern (I know . . . I asked Liz). Maybe it was the way the walls felt close and the grounds felt small, but for some reason that fact kept pressing down on me, day after day.

Don't get me wrong, it's not that I think I'm so completely kissable (because, believe me, I *don't*), but every morning I walked past the place where he had dipped me in front of the entire school. In the Grand Hall every night I ate in the exact same place where we had danced. And every day, with every step, new questions filled my mind:

- Why had Zach been in Boston (among other places)?

- What had he meant when he'd said that he was someone who didn't have anything left to lose?

- Who had set all this in motion? And why?

For three weeks I wandered the halls, wondering about people who had hurt me and a boy who hadn't tried to kiss me: two great mysteries. But there was only one of them that I had any hope of solving.

"Did you check again?" I asked Liz as we left Culture and Assimilation. "Professor Buckingham told me that MI6 registers a dozen new terrorist groups in their database every week."

"I know," Liz said. "But Cam, there's nothing there. I've run the image of that woman's ring through MI6, MI5, CIA, NSA, FBI. Believe me, if they've got initials, I've hacked them, and that image isn't anywhere."

"I didn't make that symbol up! It's got to exist . . ." I snapped, but the look that my three best friends in the world were giving made me stop short.

"Cam, darling," Bex said. "Is something . . . bothering you?"

"Well, I . . ." I started, but Macey was the one who answered.

"She's still freaked out about Zach."

I may be a pavement artist, but Macey McHenry will always know more about boys and all things boy-related than I can ever comprehend.

"What?" Macey asked with a shrug when I stared at her. "I'm intuitive." She took a step. "Plus, you talk in your sleep."

She was right. Zach and I had fallen out of that train berth together, and the world had been upside down ever since.

"Boys!" I cried, but luckily the halls were loud, and girls were hurrying, and the word got lost in the crowd. Would we ever understand them?

"He can't be . . . bad?" Liz asked softly. "I mean, didn't we establish last year that Zach is *not* bad?" She wasn't asking as a girl, she was asking as a scientist who really didn't want to reevaluate her models, duplicate her research, and change any of the things that she thought she'd once proven beyond a shadow of a doubt.

But she hadn't been on the train. She hadn't seen with her own eyes that Aunt Abby knew something about Zach. And Zach knew something about Boston. And someone knew something about that emblem. As Liz started for the labs and Macey started for Encryption, Bex and I boarded the elevator to Sublevel Two, and I couldn't help but ask, "What good is it having elite spying abilities if the people who have the highly classified information are even more elite?"

Bex smiled at me. "Because where would be the fun in that?" The spiraling ramp seemed steeper as it carried us deeper and deeper into Sublevel Two. When we reached the bottom, she stopped and looked at me. "And maybe there are some things"—she spoke slowly, and I knew the words were almost painful as she said—"we aren't supposed to know."

"Motivation," Mr. Solomon said as we settled into our chairs around the old-fashioned tables of the Covert Operations classroom. For weeks I'd been coming to that room, studying our teacher, trying to find some clue in his eyes about Zach and the train and a million other questions that swarmed my mind.

"It's why people do the things they do," our teacher said, the sentence as simple and basic as any lesson we had ever learned; and yet something in Joe Solomon's tone told me it was also the most important.

"*What*, ladies"—he took a step, scanning the dim room—"is almost always tied to *why*. There are six reasons anyone does anything: Love. Faith. Greed. Boredom. Fear . . ." he said, ticking them off on his fingers; but he lingered on the last, drawing a deep breath before he said, "Revenge."

I thought about the people on the rooftop, wondered which of those six things had brought them there. And why.

"We have gadgets," Mr. Solomon said. "We have comms units and trackers and satellites that can photograph the wings of a fly, but make no mistake, we practice a very old art. Six things, ladies. And they haven't changed in five thousand years."

Mr. Solomon turned back to the board. My classmates sat at attention, but my mind was spinning, going over and over what my teacher had just said. I gripped the edge of the table. I saw the classroom fade away. The world came into focus as I said the words, I must have known for weeks but only just realized.

"They're old."

"What are you going on about?" Bex asked. For once in her life she could barely keep up with me as I stepped from the elevator and started up the Grand Staircase.

"We were wrong. I was wrong," I said, the words coming faster now.

"Cam, what—"

"Of course Liz didn't find it in the computer files. Going back fifty years wouldn't help. Going back a hundred wouldn't help. Bex, they're not a *new* threat!"

In the foyer below us, girls were going in for lunch. The halls were alive with the smells of lasagna and talk of midterms, but my best friend and I were alone in the Hall of History as I pointed to our school's most sacred treasure.

"They're old."

Chapter Twenty-two

"That's it," I mumbled, staring at the book on the table in front of me. "I've walked by that sword a million times. I should have realized as soon as we got back. I should have recognized it on the rooftop. I should have . . . I'm an idiot!"

"It's okay, Cam," Liz soothed. "You were all . . . *concussiony*."

"Thanks," I said, even though it didn't help as much as it should have.

I looked at the etching in the ancient book. Every new student in the history of our school had heard the story of Gillian Gallagher and stared at that very image, but that day I didn't look at President Lincoln or the dozens of men who stood around him. I didn't even look at the young woman with the sword, who was moving through the ballroom with more grace and strength than a hoopskirt was ever supposed to allow.

This time I looked at the man on the floor, a pistol

falling from his limp hand, the empty scabbard at his side. This time I stared at the tiny emblem I'd seen a million times in the sword's hilt, barely visible next to Gilly's hand.

"That's it," I said softly, shifting the book to better catch the light.

Liz read the caption out loud: "Gillian Gallagher slays Joseph Cavan, founder of the Circle of Cavan. Virginia, December, 1864."

"She killed him with his own sword," Bex said in awe.

Then I dropped a satellite photo onto the open book. "The Circle of Cavan attempt to kidnap Macey McHenry, Massachusetts, present day."

"So the Circle of Cavan . . ." Liz started.

"Is alive and well," Bex finished.

I looked at my roommates. "And they want our friend."

I knew the first attempt to kill President Lincoln had really happened. I'd walked by the sword and thought of Gilly a dozen times a day for years, but before that moment Gilly's story had seemed like some fabulous dream. So, standing in the library, the fire crackling beside us, I couldn't shake the feeling that we'd just seen a dragon in the lake, a ghost in the labs. An ancient evil was alive in the world. I knew that Gilly had won the battle in the ballroom that night, and almost immediately she'd started her school, maybe because she understood the war was far from over.

"You don't think they're after Macey because she's . . ." Liz started. "You know . . ." She dropped her voice to a whisper. *"Gilly's descendant?"*

I thought about the day, more than a year before, when my mother had shared that information. And when I looked at Bex, the expression on our faces said the exact same thing: *Absolutely.*

The people on the roof had reason to hate the school and reason to hate Gilly. Macey was the last true Gallagher Girl—their best chance at real revenge.

I looked at the satellite photo again, the grainy black-and-white image that had been on my mind for weeks, and I thought about what Bex and Aunt Abby had said: The woman on the roof had been too good at her job to wear a ring that would allow her to be identified. But now I knew that's exactly why she'd worn it. I thought of the look on Abby's face as I'd studied that image in her room, and I realized my aunt had known that all along.

For the first time in a long time, a lot of things made sense.

But that didn't mean I had to like it.

From that point on, everything—and I do mean *everything*—about our school looked different.

The Gallagher Academy history section of the library? Full of books that didn't tell the whole story. That painting of Gilly standing at a window, staring across our walls? Now I had a whole different idea of what our school's founder had feared seeing in the distance.

By the end of the week, I hadn't heard a word my teachers had said without reading between some imaginary line, biting back some question that I knew they would probably never answer: Who, exactly, were the Circle of Cavan? What did they want? Where had they been for the last hundred and fifty years? And, most important, as Liz and Bex fell into step beside me on our way to dinner that Friday night, what were we supposed to tell Macey?

Because, believe it or not, "Oh, by the way, you know the guy Gilly killed? Well, I guess he's still got friends who are really ticked off about it, and they're trying to take their revenge out on you. Oh, and did we mention that you're Gilly's great-great-granddaughter, and that's why you were admitted to the school in the first place?" was harder to work into everyday conversation than you might think.

"Is khabar ko kisi kitab ke andar daal dein, ya aisa kuch?" Liz whispered as we practiced our Hindi and ate our macaroni and cheese (the gourmet kind); and yet, as much as I appreciated Liz's flash cards, I didn't think planting the news in Macey's textbook was the best way to tell her the truth.

"Usse apne pariwar ke panch jani dushmano ke naam puchain aur phir ek naam aur jord dein." Bex offered, but I shook my head because the "Hey, Macey, just when you thought no one could hate your family more than you do" option didn't seem like the way to go either.

The truth of the matter is, we might know fourteen different languages, but when it comes to breaking bad news, not even a Gallagher Girl can always find the words.

"Maybe," I said slowly and in English, despite the teachers that roamed the Grand Hall making sure our Hindi had the accent we were all trying to master, "maybe we shouldn't . . ."

"Tell her?" Liz asked, reading my mind.

I don't like keeping secrets, which, given my chosen profession, is strange but true. But I remembered the way I had felt on my first elevator ride from Sublevel Two—that there are some secrets we keep because we can't bear to let them out, and some because it's better to keep them in. I looked at my two best friends and wondered which kind we were keeping now.

"I'd want to know," Bex said simply, and I nodded, not surprised, but glad to hear it all the same.

"I . . ." Liz whispered and leaned closer. "I think . . ." she stammered again, and I could tell that Liz the genius knew that the more information you had—the more data points you could plot—the better your conclusions. But Liz the *girl,* knew that ignorance is sometimes bliss.

"No," she said finally with a shake of her head. "I wouldn't want to know. And besides"—she looked at me, her blue eyes wide—"if it were best for Macey to know, wouldn't your mom and Abby and Mr. Solomon and everybody . . . *tell her?*"

I hate it when she's right. And unfortunately, it happens a lot.

I felt Bex and Liz staring at me, and I knew that I was the tiebreaking vote. A girl at the senior table held a copy of a newspaper; it rustled as she turned the page. The headline, "Tuesday's Presidential Race Too Close to Call," screamed louder than the voices of a hundred chattering girls as Macey walked through the doors at the back of the room with the rest of the ninth graders who had stayed late in P&E. She was smiling; she was laughing; the girl by the lake seemed farther away, and yet I knew that she was still inside Macey somewhere, and I really didn't want to see her again.

"What's up?" Macey asked as she took the seat beside me. I didn't have a clue what to say or how to say it.

Fortunately, Joe Solomon was the one who answered, "Pop quiz."

"Now, I know some of you aren't on the CoveOps track of study," Mr. Solomon said, glancing down the table at the entire junior class, "but there are aspects of this life—of this world—from which you can never walk away. Ever. The fact that almost everything you say to almost everyone you love for the rest of your life will be a lie is one of them. So, if you don't mind a little extra work . . ." he said, looking down at Liz, which is kind of like asking *me* if I didn't mind an extra dessert, "plain clothes. Foyer. Twenty minutes."

Ten minutes later I was running down the Grand Stairs, a half step behind Bex and Liz. The adrenaline that only comes from going someplace else, doing something else, being someone else for just a little while was starting to course through me again. Macey was beside me. I didn't have a clue where we were going, but to be honest, I didn't care.

Abby was standing by the door, smiling a knowing, mischievous smile to everyone who passed. But as Macey and

I stepped toward the door, my aunt's smile was totally not what we got.

An arm. That's what I saw first. An arm blocking the doorway, reaching for Macey's shoulder.

"Sorry," Aunt Abby said. "Not a secure location."

I gave Macey a sympathetic shrug and tried to push past. But Abby didn't budge. "Oh." She looked at me. "I think you and your mother have an . . . arrangement?"

I could hear the retreating footsteps in the blackness outside. I could feel the opportunity slipping away.

"But—" I started. I didn't know if I was pleading with my aunt, or my teacher, or with Macey's Secret Service shadow, but I knew the situation called for some serious pleading with *someone*. "But this is an assignment!" I blurted. Abby just shook her head.

"Sorry, girls," she said. "Sure"—she glanced at Macey—"I'll take a bullet for you, but that doesn't mean I'll incur the wrath of Rachel."

Bex and Liz skidded to a stop outside and turned back to us, Bex's eyes asking what was taking us so long; but Aunt Abby turned away, into the darkness, without a second glance.

"Hey," I said, running to catch up with Macey. "You okay?"

She smiled. "I'm great." But she didn't sound great. Not even a little.

"It's me you're talking to," I told her. "I can't vote, remember?"

"I'm . . ." This time she really seemed to be thinking

194

about the answer, and I knew there was a chance I'd get the truth instead of the party line. "I'm mad," she said finally, the words echoing down the long empty hall.

"Okay."

"And I'm sick of this." She held out the cast that covered her left arm. "This stupid, dirty, itchy . . . *reminder*. But apparently I poll ten points better with it on."

"Okay."

"And I'm so tired . . ." Her voice was softer then, her fight almost gone as she sank to the stairs. "I am so tired of being Macey McHenry."

I sank onto the stairs beside her.

"It could be worse," I tried, hoping my smile didn't look quite as counterfeit as it felt. "You could be left-handed," I said, pointing to the cast on her left arm.

Macey laughed. "I could be stuck on a campaign bus . . . with my mother."

"You could *be* your mother," I tried.

"I could be Preston," she said with a laugh.

I thought about it for a second. If Macey was going crazy living in the most secure building in the country, with Aunt Abby as her security detail, then the son of a presidential candidate had to be going out of his mind.

"I'm so ready for this to be over," she said as if she'd just admitted her deepest, darkest secret. "I'm so ready for Tuesday."

That was the moment we'd been waiting for—the opening I'd needed to tell her the truth about what was happening and warn her that it wouldn't end that quickly—that she wasn't going to stop being Gilly's descendant on Wednesday.

"What?" she asked, reading my face. I'd come to that corridor to tell her the truth, to warn her, but Macey still had hope that Tuesday might mark the end, and I for one didn't want to take that away from her too soon.

I found myself standing, thinking, moving.

"What do you want to do, Macey?" I asked.

"I want . . . I want to not be watched all the time," she said. "I don't want to be looked at by the people in town. I don't want to be looked at by my parents. I just don't want to be"—she turned her gaze toward me—"looked at."

When you look like Macey McHenry, the urge to disappear might sound crazy. But not if you're a teenage girl. Not if you've been on the cover of every magazine in America in the last six months. And not if you're a chameleon.

I was maybe the one person in the world who could understand, and maybe that's why she told me.

And maybe that's why I said, "Come on."

Chapter twenty-three

Did I know it was against the rules? Yes.

Did I think it was foolish? Absolutely.

Did I think it was worth it? Honestly? Yeah, I guess I did.

Sometimes I wonder what makes me the Chameleon—why I like to hide and blend, why I'd rather be unseen than noticed. But as Macey and I walked down the basement hallway, I knew that being invisible was not without its appeal.

After all, it had taken ninety minutes, but Macey McHenry had been successfully made under (not over), and now we were ready for the outside world. I glanced at the girl beside me. Her trademark blue eyes were hidden behind brown contacts and thick glasses. We'd added a faint trace of freckles across her pale nose. Her glossy black hair was tucked up under a curly red wig, and I knew that's all anyone who glanced at her would remember: big red hair and glasses.

I reached for the old Gallagher family tapestry that hung against the stone wall, then looked at the girl I hardly recognized, and said, "You sure?"

She reached for the small crest that was inset into the stone and twisted the sword, triggering the release of one of my favorite secret passageways. "You bet."

Roseville always struck me as the kind of place where nothing ever really changes, but that night, lights burned in the distance, and a bright iridescent glow grew from the horizon as Macey and I walked into town. There was a sound, too, that came and went, a low rumbling, like a river. All around us, people were hurrying from restaurants, carrying big armloads of blankets across the square, streaming toward the light.

"What do you want to do?" I turned to Macey. She was looking at a reflection in a store window of two girls. To the citizens of Roseville they probably looked like ordinary girls. People passed them by without a second look. The redhead in the glass was no one of consequence. She was unnoticed and unseen.

She was like me.

And she was loving every second of it as she said, "We follow them."

Okay, as a pavement artist, it wasn't the toughest tail I'd ever encountered. The lights were strong and growing brighter. Dozens of people were walking in the same direction, down the side streets that led from the square.

A pair of men were passing, arguing.

"McHenry," one of the men spat at the other. "He's no better than the others."

I looked at Macey, expecting to see some sort of reaction in her eyes, but her expression was as indifferent as someone would expect a sixteen-year-old girl's to be.

"I don't care if he does have ties to Roseville!" one of the men protested.

"You mean his daughter being up at the school?" the other man asked.

And then Macey did something I'll never forget. She bumped into the man, actually made physical contact, and looked him in the eye. I held my breath for a second as Macey McHenry—the very girl he was talking about—stared at him with her contact-colored eyes and said, "Excuse me."

"No, pardon me, young lady," the guy said, and then he turned back to his friend. He kept walking toward the lights.

I knew we were breaking a promise to my mother, and that we were taking a terrible risk. But the look on Macey's face right then made it all okay.

Then we turned a corner, and I saw the rows of glowing orbs, the waving American flag, and I heard the roaring sound for what it was. Not a river . . .

Football.

The Roseville football stadium was on the far side of town, nestled against the tall hills that rose from the valley just fifty yards behind me. In the distance, the band started playing. The sound echoed through the hills. The cheering crowd grew louder as we walked toward the chain-link fence, joining the stream of people that flowed inside the gates. Steel beams framed the stands. Specks of dust and debris would fall sometimes like a faint snowfall as we stood beneath the bleachers, staring out onto the field. There were uniformed officials holding big orange markers. A coach paced back and forth, yelling orders no one seemed to hear. Cheerleaders moved in perfect unison, their red pleated skirts flipping as they yelled and kicked. And behind them sat a small stage with five girls in crowns and fancy dresses.

"Oh my gosh," Macey said, pointing to the girl in the center who wore a white dress and a tiara. She sounded as overwhelmed as I felt.

"I think maybe she's their queen," I guessed, because, honestly, we were in completely foreign territory!

Spies have to be comfortable in all kinds of social situations, but I don't think I'd ever been anywhere where some people were wearing tiaras and others were wearing sweatshirts. I mean, I'd watched football on TV with Grandpa Morgan, but never once had I seen any girls in formal wear!

A track circled around the football field. On the other side lay the opposing stands, the opposing team. Macey and I started walking in that direction, past the concession stand, and ran right into Tina Walters.

"Excuse me," Tina said, stumbling a little. And then she looked at Macey. She looked at me. She opened her mouth to speak, but then, just as quickly, she shook her head as if dismissing some crazy thought.

"Ummm . . . sorry." I grabbed Macey and bolted away.

Macey looked at me, her contact-colored eyes wide as we both silently mouthed, *Pop quiz!*

Near the bathrooms we saw Eva Alvarez posing as a member of the other team's flag corps and talking to a middle-aged woman wearing an I ♥ #32 corsage that was as large as her head.

I heard Courtney Bauer's laughter from under the stands. Now I know, technically speaking, that a crowd full of Gallagher Girls is supposed to make me feel safe, but right then they weren't backup—they were highly trained operatives who could blow our cover at any time.

Macey and I stayed calm and kept walking, taking in the sights and sounds, until suddenly things felt . . . different. Again. I sensed the Gallagher Girls in the crowd, but also . . . something else. The game must have been going well for Roseville, because the home crowd was cheering; but for some reason I found myself thinking about another day and another crowd. But this time I didn't think I was crazy as my mind flashed back to Washington, D.C. This time, I knew what I was looking for.

"He's here," I muttered as my gaze swept over the crowd, no longer seeing football fans and cheerleaders, band members and aging former jocks.

"What?" Macey asked over the roar of the crowd.

"Zach," I whispered back.

"I *don't know* why he didn't kiss you!" Macey said with an exasperated sigh, as if she totally wasn't in the mood to debrief again.

"No." I shook my head. "He's *here*."

And that got my roommate's attention. "How do you know?" she asked, turning to take in the crowd. "Is it a pavement artist thing?"

"No," I said. "It's a girl thing."

Macey nodded as if she knew exactly what I was feeling. She scanned the bleachers. "Maybe Blackthorne is here for a CoveOps exercise too?" she offered, but I shook my head. "Ooh! Solomon alert!" Macey said then, coming even more alive.

Our teacher was by the flagpole. Our teacher was looking our way. It would have been easy to spin around, to try to hide. But luckily Macey stayed with me, quiet and still, as Joe Solomon's gaze passed over us.

Maybe it was instinct or training that made me freeze. Or maybe it was the sight of the boy standing forty feet behind my teacher, in the middle of the track, staring right at me.

Being recognized during a covert operation is bad. We're talking democracy (not to mention life) as you know it may cease to exist . . . bad. Enemy agents might try to kill you. Friends who don't have a clue that you're posing as a United Nations translator and using the name Tiffany St. James might totally blow your cover. But until that moment,

I didn't realize just how dangerous it is to be recognized by . . .

Your ex-boyfriend.

"Isn't that . . ." Macey started, but I couldn't wait for her to finish.

"Josh."

My mind raced with all the reasons I shouldn't panic. After all, it was homecoming and it seemed like the entire town of Roseville had come out for the show. And not only that, but at that moment I looked more like Macey than like me as I stood there in my long black wig and blue contacts, and jeans that the real me would never wear for fun on a Friday night. But the hope I clung to the hardest, as I stood twenty feet away from my first boyfriend, was simple: I was still the girl nobody sees.

But there had always been one exception to that rule. And he was standing right in front of me.

"Has he . . . filled out a little?" Macey asked, squinting her eyes to see better through her fake glasses. "He seems . . . hotter," she added, as if she totally approved.

I wanted to say no. I wanted to pretend it didn't matter. But when he turned and started walking away from us, I did what any spy (not to mention ex-girlfriend) would do: I followed him.

I should have waited for Macey, but instead I found myself pushing through the marching band, which was lining up to take the field at halftime. I headed after the boy who was walking freely through the crowd—not hiding. No disguise. I marveled at the fact that there are boys in the world who are exactly what they seem.

From a pavement artist standpoint, following a boy like Josh Abrams is about as easy as it gets. After all, he's untrained, unaware, and utterly unconcerned about the *Essentials of Elementary Countersurveillance* (my favorite book when I was seven). And yet, something about that mission was harder than anything I'd done in a long time. Maybe it was the fact that I was on totally unfamiliar ground. Maybe it was the way the crowds crushed around me, making it difficult to follow against the current. Or maybe it was the sight of another boy who had come from nowhere and now stood blocking my path.

"What are you doing here, Gallagher Girl?" Zach's voice was low but strong. He gripped my forearm and ushered me out of the way of a convertible that was driving the freshman homecoming attendant around the track.

"CoveOps assignment," I lied. "You?"

"I thought you weren't supposed to leave school," he told me.

"Yeah, because *you're* so into sticking around campus these days. Seriously, Zach, do you ever stay at Blackthorne?"

But he didn't answer (which, Macey tells me, is a typical reaction for both boys and spies, so I don't know which he was being then).

"I had a feeling you might try something like this." It sounded like the most truthful thing he'd said to me in ages.

"Just tell me . . ." Zach started, and for the first time his anger seemed to fade. "Just tell me you didn't do this to see Jimmy."

"Josh," I corrected Zach for about the millionth time, but he didn't smile, and somehow I knew that the joke was long since over. "No," I said, meaning it. "I'm just . . . here."

I didn't look for him, but somehow I knew that Josh was standing with a group of friends ten feet away. Zach was right in front of me. There I was, caught between two boys who couldn't have been more different. If I'd been another girl with another cover, I don't know what I would have done; but right then, only one thing mattered.

"Why were you in Boston, Zach?" The air was crisp and cool around us. Soft music started on the loudspeaker as the homecoming court made their way to the center of the field. I felt more than a new season blowing in the breeze, so maybe that's why I looked at the boy I hadn't really seen in months and said, "Why are you here, Zach?"

I stepped closer to him, waiting for him to reach out, to tease, to smile. And more than anything, I wanted him to say *I am here for you.*

The space between us shrank, but as I took another step forward, Zach took a step back. Last spring, he'd teased me, he'd flirted with me—I'd been the one who was hard to get. But standing under those bright lights, I could see that somehow, in the last few months, Zach and I had changed places. I didn't like the game from that side of the field.

"Come on," he said, taking my hand (but not in a nice, romantic way). "We're taking Macey home."

"*We're* not doing anything."

"Fine," he said, starting away. "*I'll* go find Solomon, get his opinion."

"Zach," I started, cutting him off, but he wheeled on me.

"Do you even know who's out there?" he snapped louder now, and then just as quickly he stepped closer. "Do you even care?"

"The Circle of Cavan is after my sisterhood, Zach. Not yours. They're hunting my friends. They're sending Gallagher Girls down laundry chutes, so don't show up here and lecture me about what's at stake." He drew a breath as if to speak, but I knew better than to let him. "If Ioseph Cavan's followers want to settle the score with Gillian Gallagher's great-great-granddaughter, then they're going to deal with all of us, and that doesn't necessarily include you."

The announcer was talking over the loudspeaker, saying something about the homecoming queen and her deep love of puppies or something, but I just looked at Zach, trying to shake the feeling that I hadn't really seen him in months. If ever. "Why do I feel like I can't trust you anymore?"

I wanted him to lash out. I wanted him to fight, to protest, to argue—to do anything but look deeper into my eyes and say, "Because the Gallagher Academy doesn't admit fools."

Hundreds of people filled the stands around us. They were teachers and accountants, stay-at-home moms and men who worked at the toilet paper factory—regular people doing their best to live regular lives. They couldn't have been farther from Macey McHenry (both the spy and the girl) if they'd tried.

And yet she was right there beside them.

Beside us.

And she'd heard everything we'd said.

"The family tie to Roseville," Macey softly repeated what the man on the street had said.

"Macey," I said, stepping closer.

"Does this mean . . ." she started, and I knew there were a dozen ways that sentence could have ended. If I had just discovered that I was related to Gillian Gallagher, I would have been ecstatic. Bex would have thought it was the coolest thing ever. Liz might have decided to conduct some serious DNA experiments to determine if covertness was hereditary.

But it didn't matter what *we* would have done. What really mattered was what Macey *did*.

"You knew about this?" she asked me. Her voice was cracking. Her lip was shaking. "How long have you known about this?"

I could have lied, I guess. But I didn't. Maybe because Macey had lived with me for over a year and would see through it. Maybe because we hadn't covered lying to a trained operative yet in CoveOps. Or maybe I just thought Macey had the right to know that of the thousands of Gallagher Girls in the world, she was the only one who carried Gilly's blood in her veins.

"Yeah, my mom told us last—"

"Us!" Macey snapped. "Does the whole school know?"

"No! Just Bex and Liz and me. Mom explained all that after you got accepted. She—"

"So I'm Gillian Gallagher's descendant?" The fire seemed to be fading from her, so I reached out, still half afraid that when I touched her she would turn to ash. "So *that's* why they let me in."

"Macey, it's not—"

"True?" she said, staring at me, but for once in my life I couldn't lie—couldn't hide. I could only watch as she pushed away without another word, through the red-clad members of the Pride of Roseville Marching Band, who were exiting the field.

"Macey!" I called after her, but then Zach's hand was in mine.

"Cam—" he started.

"Not now, Zach." I jerked away. Maybe I wanted to find Macey. Or maybe I just wanted to be anywhere but there.

I set off through the crowd, pushing through the band and out into open space—seeing potential threats everywhere I turned.

Twenty feet to my right and up three rows, there was a guy in a red cap who jumped to his feet to cheer a split second too late, as if his attention had been elsewhere. On the track between the cheerleaders and the bleachers, two women stood together scanning the crowd while wearing shoes that no small-town housewife would be caught dead in.

I wanted to scream into my comms unit and call for backup, but I had no comms. There was no backup. And Macey was already gone.

Chapter twenty-four

The road from Roseville had never felt so long. In the hours that passed, the mansion had never felt so big. And I had never felt so stupid as when Bex and Liz and I went room to room, floor to floor, searching for Macey.

Covert Operations Report
0500 hours

Operatives Morgan, Baxter, and Sutton conducted a detailed search of the Gallagher Mansion, following the textbook grid pattern of detection. (They were sure about this because Operative Sutton brought along the actual textbook.)

"I know she made it back," I said for what must have been the hundredth time, but I had to keep saying the words. It didn't matter that neither Bex nor Liz needed to hear them. "I tracked her footprints down the tunnel. . . . She came back that way—I'm sure of it. She left her wig by the door with the rest of her disguise, so I dropped mine there too and went looking for her. . . ." I looked at Bex and Liz, not even trying to hide my panic as I begged them to believe me. "I know she made it back!"

I wanted Liz to cite the incredible odds in our favor that Macey was fine. I expected Bex to tell me that everything was going to be okay, but instead she just stared at me and asked, "Scale of one to ten, how mad was she?"

We were in the library, but there were no girls among the stacks. The clock in my head was telling me it was almost five in the morning. The fire in the fireplace was nothing but a pile of smoldering embers—the only light in the room. I thought about Bex's question, slowly realizing that mad wasn't the word. Mad could be handled by challenging Bex to a good sparring match in the P&E barn. Mad goes away with a good night's sleep.

"Not mad," I said, shaking my head. "It was more like she was—"

"Heartbroken." Liz's voice was so soft I barely heard it, and even now I'm not sure if she knew she'd said the word aloud. We'd been looking for Macey for hours, but something in the way she sank onto the spiraling staircase made me realize that, somewhere along the way, Liz had gone missing too.

"When Macey found out, she was heartbroken," Liz said again, and I knew she was right.

"Yeah," I said, turning to her. "Heartbroken."

"Oh, I'll break something when we find her. . . ." Bex's accent was coming back in waves. "She's gonna get herself snatched right up if she keeps acting this bloody stupid. Running about the country on her own . . ."

"You don't get it, do you?" It was the first time I'd ever heard Liz raise her voice, the first time I'd seen her skin so deathly white. Even Bex stopped and stared. "I mean, look at you—look at both of you! You don't know what it's like. You . . . *belong*," Liz said, as if Bex and I were at the core of an ancient secret and didn't realize it. And I guess, in a way, we were.

"You." Liz turned to Bex. "You go all over the world with your mom and dad, tracking down arms dealers and staking out terrorists during summer break."

Bex started to protest until she realized that what Liz was saying wasn't an insult and, furthermore, it was absolutely true.

"And you," Liz said, spinning on me. "Cam, your mom is the headmistress . . . Your aunt's a living legend. . . ." For some reason I felt my cheeks flush red. "You guys don't have any idea what it's like to be . . . normal. And then one day someone tells you that the toughest, most elite, most amazing school in the world is in Roseville, Virginia"—Liz's voice had taken on a very dreamy quality, but as she settled her gaze on us, her words turned to steel—"and they want *you*."

I thought about what she'd said and realized that there'd never been a moment in my life when I'd doubted whether or not I could become a Gallagher Girl. For Bex, the toughest barrier was geography.

"Yeah," Liz said, reading our expressions. "I'd always been pretty good at school." It was probably the understatement of the century, but I didn't dare interrupt. "People always told *me* I was smart—people always said that *I* was special. But Macey . . ." Liz's voice cracked. My eyes were going blurry, and even Bex looked as if she were about to cry. "What have people always told *her?*"

I didn't want to think about the answer to that question—not then. Not ever. So the three of us sat surrounded by books and secrets and the light of a dying fire, finally realizing that we were the only people in Macey's life who knew not to judge a girl by her cover.

"We've got to find her," Bex said, starting for the door. "Now."

But I was already way ahead of her, pushing forward, riding a wave of exhaustion and terror; instinct driving me forward as I prayed that I was wrong.

I could hear them following behind me, their footsteps echoing on the old stone floors while Bex called, "We've looked down there already."

But I just ran faster through the abandoned halls, past empty classrooms and dark windows and, finally, down the stairs that led to the long basement corridor—to the place where, in a way, it had all begun.

There were no windows there. The corridor was dark, the stone floors were rough, but still I ran toward the place where my mother had brought us more than a year ago and told us the truth about Macey.

As I stopped in front of the tapestry that showed the entire Gallagher Family tree, I tried to imagine how many times I'd disappeared behind it, but I knew that our trip that night had been the most important journey that that passageway had ever witnessed.

I was breathing heavily, almost afraid of what I'd find, as Bex and Liz appeared beside me.

"She's here somewhere," Liz said. "She's got to be. She's . . ."

But I wasn't really listening as I pulled the tapestry aside and turned the tiny sword in the Gallagher Academy crest, which lay embedded in the stone wall.

"She might be in the ninth-grade common room," Liz was saying in the manner of someone who has to keep talking or else she'll fall asleep. "They have those really comfy chairs. . . ."

But I just watched the wall slide aside to reveal the empty corridor. I listened to the sounds of silence echo through the shaft. I looked down at the place where Macey and I had left our disguises earlier that night—at the place where no wigs, no glasses, no trace of the girls we'd been earlier that night remained.

"She's here," Liz said. "She can't be . . ."

"Gone."

Chapter twenty-five

"Tell me." Mr. Solomon's voice was steady as he sat on the coffee table in front of the leather couch in my mother's office. I didn't look around the room. I didn't listen as my mother spoke on one phone and my aunt on another. I didn't watch Liz and Bex as they sat in the window seat, answering questions from Buckingham and Mr. Smith. It was the quietest chaos I'd ever seen or heard, so I just sat there, trying to keep my tired mind from drifting too far down that empty passageway, chasing after Macey.

One floor below us, girls were gathering for Saturday morning breakfast; up in the suites, half the junior class was probably sleeping in. The news about Macey hadn't spread yet, but it would . . . and I knew it was up to the people in my mother's office to make sure it didn't spread too far; so maybe that's why Joe Solomon looked at me as if we were the only two people in the room—the school. His world wasn't falling apart. He was going to hold it together—I could hold it together. I just had to . . .

"Tell me *everything*, Ms. Morgan."

"The last time I saw her was last night."

"Everything."

"At eight forty-seven p.m. last night we were in town . . . at the football game," I admitted, expecting him to shout or at least look confused, but Joe Solomon isn't one of the best covert operatives in the world for nothing, so he just nodded and told me to go on. "And we saw Zach."

Maybe it was my overactive imagination, but I could have sworn that *that* made Mr. Solomon blink. I thought about the way he and Zach had rendezvoused in the train tunnel in Philadelphia. A dozen questions sprung to mind, but as badly as I wanted answers, I wanted Macey back more. So I said, "Do you want it verbatim?"

He seemed to appreciate the offer but shook his head. "Not now."

"Zach and I were talking about the Circle of Cavan—I figured it out, you know. From the ring and the sword?"

He smiled. "I knew you would. Go on."

"Macey overheard us. She didn't know she was related to Gilly. She wanted to know if that was why she was admitted here. She didn't know about any of it until then, and so she . . . ran. It was loud and crowded and I lost her." I couldn't look at him. "I'm supposed to be a pavement artist, and I lost her."

"It's what she does, Ms. Morgan." Mr. Solomon's eyes found mine, but there was a change in him somehow. "Running," he added. "Of course, technically, her pattern is to do something to get kicked out, but that's not an option now, so she's taken matters into her own hands. Do you know what I'm saying, Ms. Morgan?"

But sadly, I didn't.

"Sometimes people run . . . to see if you'll come after them."

I've seen Joe Solomon every school day for more than a year, but I don't think I'll ever really know him. There are times when he's one of the strongest people I've ever known, and then there are moments—like that one—when I think he might be broken, deep down, in a place that will never mend.

And then just like that, he became my teacher again. "Is anything missing from your room?"

I stopped for a second, closed my eyes, and visualized the space. "Her passport."

"No clothes? No money?"

"She has fourteen different credit cards and knows all the numbers by heart."

Mr. Solomon looked as if he wanted to smile, as if he wanted to laugh. "She also has the most famous face in the country right now, Ms. Morgan," he told me, not a hint of worry in his voice. "I think we can track her down." But then he read my expression, and the smile slid from his lips. "What?"

"Well," I said slowly, "remember how we had that disguise class?"

There wasn't time for yelling. It wasn't the place for mother-daughter lessons in regret. As our teachers huddled around us, I gave them details of the items Macey had taken with her. When I finished, my mother shook her head and started for the phone. Unfortunately, Aunt Abby wasn't as easily distracted.

"I know what I did," I said before my aunt could utter a word.

"Do you?" There was something deeper in her eyes. She wasn't just Aunt Abby then; she was more than Macey's protector; for a split second she was the woman on the train, but then—just as quickly—that woman was gone. "You went into town alone and . . . and now, come Tuesday, we are going to have to produce Macey McHenry, and if we can't, every agent in the Secret Service and half the FBI is going to descend upon this mansion, Cameron, and I don't know if even your mother can keep them out. They're going to pull back carpets and knock down doors until they track Macey's every step, and in the process, they might take my head for good measure. And meanwhile, she's—" Abby placed a hand on her hip, and for the first time, I saw a holster. Like smoke and fire, I knew that somewhere there was a gun. "She's out there. She's goodness only knows—"

"New York!" Buckingham shouted and banged down a phone. "A young woman matching Macey's description purchased a bus ticket to New York last night. And someone using one of Macey's mother's business accounts reserved a private jet to Switzerland."

Abby looked at me. "Her family has a house there," I said. "It fits."

Mom turned to Buckingham. "We have alumni in Switzerland?"

"Of course," was Buckingham's reply.

"Have them sit on her until we can get a grab team in place." Professor Buckingham turned to go, but Mom called after her. "And Patricia, tell them she's a hard target. Tell them she's one of us."

I would have given anything for Macey to have heard that. Maybe then she would have believed me. Maybe then she wouldn't have run away. Maybe then things would have been very different. But Macey didn't hear, and that was the problem. She was half a world away. On her own. And one look at my mother's worried eyes told me that we probably weren't the only ones looking for her.

As Abby bolted for the door, Bex, Liz, and I rushed after her.

"When do we leave?" Bex said.

"*We* aren't going anywhere," Abby snapped. Through the windows I could see that a chopper was already spinning its blades, waiting for her. She rushed toward the staircase, but then stopped short. "She'll be okay, you know." For a second, Abby was her old self as she cocked a hip. "Trust me."

I know, scientifically speaking, that all days have twenty-four hours. One thousand four hundred and forty minutes. Eighty-six thousand, four hundred seconds. But even Liz admitted that the days that followed seemed longer, as we stared out every window we passed, expecting the gates to swing open, to see Aunt Abby and Macey coming down the lane.

But the gates stayed closed. The lane stayed empty. And Macey stayed gone.

By Monday night, a feeling was resurfacing inside of me like a virus that had been dormant for years, as I thought about when my parents would go away for days or weeks on end; before the days when I knew my father wasn't coming back at all. Walking downstairs for supper, I couldn't shake the feeling that I'm really great at disappearing, but Macey might have been a whole different kind of gone.

"Oops, sorry," someone said, just as I looked up to see Tina Walters running up the stairs. The sign above the Grand Hall told me we were going to be conversing that night in Portuguese; the aromas that filled the foyer told me we were having lasagna. But something in the way Tina looked at me told me that none of the junior class was feeling very hungry.

"You okay, Cam?" she asked, and I nodded, but for some reason I couldn't move out of her way.

"Tina, have you . . ." I started, then paused because I honestly couldn't quite believe what I was about to ask. "Have your sources heard anything?"

I wanted her to tell me that Macey was okay. I would have settled for a crazy story about a girl matching Macey's description who had been staking out an ex-KGB hitman in Bucharest. I needed anything but the sight of Tina shaking her head and saying, "Not a word."

She smiled sympathetically. "But no news can be good news, right?" she asked. "Everyone's looking for her."

But as I looked up into the Hall of History, all I could do was stare at the sword that still stood gleaming inside its case, a sharp blade cutting through time, and whisper, "That's what I'm afraid of."

I'm an expert on hiding. Not to brag, but it's true, and as I sat staring at my plate that night, something about Macey's disappearance didn't make sense.

"Both disguises," I said.

"What?" Bex asked, leaning closer.

"Both disguises were gone when we went back—the one she wore and the one I wore."

Then Bex grinned at me. "You thinking what I'm thinking?" she asked, and in a flash we were running up the stairs, Liz trailing along behind us.

The Hall of History was dim. My mother's office door was closed, but I didn't slow down until Madame Dabney appeared out of nowhere, firmly blocking my path.

"I need to see my mom," I blurted.

"Oh, Cammie dear, I'm afraid your mother isn't here."

"But I need to see her!"

"Well, I don't doubt that, but given recent circumstances, the headmistress has gone to see Senator and Mrs. McHenry to explain why their daughter might be . . . delayed . . . in attending the campaign's watch party tomorrow night. That is, if we get her back from Switzerland in time at all,"

Madame Dabney added just as Bex and I lurched forward.

"But Macey's not in Switzerland!" we blurted at the exact same time.

Madame Dabney stopped. She turned. "Why do you say this? What do you know?"

"Well . . ." Bex and Liz and I glanced at each other. "It's just that she took both disguises. And you've been looking for her in Switzerland for three days. I think the reason no one has found her is because she isn't there."

"Cameron, dear, I understand your concern, but a girl fitting Macey's description took a private plane to Switzerland—"

"But—" I started, but Madame Dabney didn't let me finish.

"Her passport was booked through. She's there, ladies." Madame Dabney patted my arm. "She's there. And I don't want you to worry. We'll find her."

Walking upstairs to our suite, I couldn't help but think that either Macey deserved to be called a Gallagher Girl or she didn't; that she was either good enough or she wasn't. We couldn't have it both ways, no matter what our faculty seemed to think.

I closed the door behind us and looked at Bex. "If you're Macey, what do you do?" I asked.

"I stay off the grid, for starters," Bex said, and I nodded. "Credit cards and passports are amateur hour. I don't care what grade she's technically in, Macey's no amateur."

Bex gestured as if to say it was my turn. "If I had the most recognizable face in the country and two disguises in my possession, no way I'd travel all the way to Europe without using one of them."

Bex nodded and I looked at Liz, who shrugged.

"I'm a nerd," she admitted. "I don't know CoveOps."

"You know Macey," Bex whispered, and it was maybe the truest thing any one of us had said in a very long time.

Liz settled back on her bed. I could see her flipping through the giant database that is her mind, but the answer wasn't in there—it was in her heart. So finally she took a deep breath and said, "I guess I'd just want to go someplace safe."

The mansion was quiet. I leaned against a drafty window, watching the pieces of the puzzle float through my mind until I knew they didn't quite fit. I thought about Liz's words, and the pale, ghostly look on Macey's face as we'd stood in the too-bright light of a chilly football field. Cool air washed over my arms—I saw our roommate shiver in the wind. And then . . . I knew.

"Get the keys to the Dodge, Liz," I said as I stood and started for my closet.

Bex was already gearing up—for what, it didn't matter. But Liz studied me.

"Where are we going?"

"To bring our sister home."

Chapter twenty-six

I don't think any girl in the history of the Gallagher Academy for Exceptional Young Women had ever run away from school before that weekend, but by Tuesday morning, the total had climbed to four.

While Liz slept and Bex drove, I sat in the passenger seat of the Dodge, worrying that we might not find it. After all, at the end of summer, the forest had been thick with green foliage, weeds, and tall grasses lining the narrow roads. But by November, the fields were fallow, the trees were bare, and in the pale light of dawn, the whole world seemed like a mirage, or maybe just like a very good cover, and I couldn't help but think that, spy skills or not, I had been a girl with a concussion the last time I'd been there.

Bex drove slowly down a blacktop road until, finally, I saw a gravel lane no more substantial than a trail, and said, "Turn here."

"What is this, some kind of safe house?" Bex asked as we

both squinted through the pale light and dense woods, and I thought about what our CoveOps teacher had said.

"It had better be," I said as Bex came to a stop. "Mr. Solomon owns it."

Covert Operations Report

Operatives Morgan, Baxter, and Sutton decided to proceed on foot, considering the property's owner was a highly trained security professional (in addition to being really, really hot).

Pushing through the woods, I searched for something familiar. The roof of a cabin was barely visible through the trees, but there was no smoke from the chimney—no signs of life—and a hundred doubts seemed to nag at me: What if I was wrong and this wasn't where Macey had run? What if we were too late? So I asked one question that scared me the least, "What if it isn't the right house?"

As I took another step, Bex's hand grasped my forearm, and I froze. I didn't have to look down to know that my right foot was inches away from a thin wire that would, no doubt, trigger a silent alarm. I didn't have to hear Bex say, "It's the right place," to know that it was true.

Now, normally, under ideal covert circumstances, a highly trained operative would slow down. And survey the scene. And plan a careful route, or regroup. But ideal covert circumstances hardly ever include Liz.

"Hey, what are you guys . . ." she started, and in the next instant she was stumbling over a rock with a cry of, "Oopsie daisy!"

She soared headfirst over the trip wire by my foot and landed on a pile of leaves. Bex and I lunged for her, but it was too late: gravity was taking over, and Liz was sliding down the hill, tumbling through bushes, slicing between two infrared motion sensors so perfectly that I'm sure we couldn't have duplicated the precision if we'd tried.

"She's gonna hit that—" Bex started but then couldn't finish, because instead of tumbling into a fallen log, Liz somehow managed to change direction and plow through a thicket of blackberry vines.

"Liz!" I yelled, running after her until the ground was too steep, the fallen leaves too wet with dew, and my feet flew out from under me as well. Behind me, I heard Bex gasp as she lost her footing too.

Branches whipped across my face. My hands fell wrist-deep into mud, and still I tumbled forward, faster and faster. In my mind, sirens were already sounding—a S.W.A.T. team was already on its way.

And then, finally, the tumbling stopped. I sat on the ground, covered in mud and decaying leaves. I felt nothing but my breath and the crush of Bex, who landed on top of me. I managed to wipe the mud out of my eyes, as two impossibly long legs appeared above us, and Macey McHenry said, "You're late."

The Operatives decided to take this rare opportunity to do a detailed reconnaissance of the part-time homes of trained security professionals, during which they discovered the following:

- A box of lures, rods, and hooks that could be VERY helpful in illegal interrogation tactics. (But upon closer inspection they appeared to be used for actual fishing.)
- Four plain white T-shirts
- Six pairs of tube socks
- One Swiss Army knife (that appeared to have been issued by the actual Swiss Army)
- Forty-seven maps in sixteen languages
- Zero love letters, pictures, or notebooks with doodles on the cover
- The most comprehensive first-aid kit ever assembled by man

"Cat food!" Liz cried as she peered into yet another cabinet. I heard her rushing to write it down on the list, and then she said, "I wonder what *that* means?"

I could feel Bex and Liz swarming to take in every detail of the place, marveling over the fact that the curtains were homemade and the windows weren't bulletproof. But I just stood by the narrow bed on the sleeping porch, staring at the patchwork quilt, revisiting the things that Mr. Solomon had told me there, knowing somehow that there were no answers in that little cabin. No matter how hard Liz looked, I doubted she would find a crystal ball.

Macey stood beside me. We watched our reflections in the glass and stared out at the lake. I couldn't help thinking that it had taken us a long time to walk away from the end of the pier.

Maybe Liz was right and she'd wanted someplace safe. Maybe Mr. Solomon really did understand that running was the only way Macey would find out if we'd run after her. Or maybe, like me, she just wanted to disappear for a little while.

But that didn't change the fact that we'd found her.

And we weren't the only people looking.

The screen door screeched as we stepped outside. It had taken less than three months, but somehow we'd found our way back, and I had to know if Macey was still the girl by the lake.

"Macey," I started, but before I could draw a breath, she read my mind.

"I know we can't stay."

There's something inherently safe about lake houses with CIA protection and falling leaves and contests about who can skip stones the farthest (Bex totally won, by the way). But every spy knows that things will always change. Always. And the van was waiting.

"We can go back to school, or you can go be with your parents at the watch party, but . . ." I felt myself looking for the words I feared.

"Was I that easy to track?" Macey asked, still staring out at the lake as if it were a mirror.

"No," I said, and for the first time she shot me a look. "We found you because you're way too good to get tracked with one phone call."

I sat down at the end of the pier. "Besides, you took both disguises. In one, you can look like someone else." I thought of the glossy black wig I'd worn. "In the other, the right someone else can look like you."

"From there it was easy to imagine you offering some poor, unsuspecting girl a free ride to Europe and swapping passports with her," Bex added as she and Liz walked up behind us.

"So that explains how you guessed—" Macey started.

"*Knew*," Liz corrected, unwilling to accept partial credit when she'd gotten an answer right.

"Knew," Macey went on, "I wasn't in Switzerland. How'd you find me here?"

I looked out over the lake and thought about a day not that long ago. "This is where I would have come," I said, not realizing until then that it was true.

"Me too," added Bex.

We all looked at Liz, who nodded. "Yeah."

Macey laughed. It was so quick and clean that I could have sworn it sent a ripple coursing through the lake. "Are they really still searching in Switzerland?"

"By now they've widened the net to include half of Northern Europe," Bex said with a grin.

"Still think they only let you in because of who your family is?" I asked.

"Yes." Macey's answer shocked me. I'd been in the process of getting up. The coarse wood of the dock was pinching my hands as they supported too much of my weight, and yet I couldn't move.

Macey smiled. She cocked an eyebrow and said, "But that's not why they keep me."

Of all the tests Macey McHenry had passed in the last year, there wasn't a doubt in my mind that that was the biggest one.

"Besides," she said playfully batting her eyes, "my father is potentially the second most powerful man in the country."

"Well," Liz said softly, "not for much longer."

"Why?" I asked, looking at her.

"Because the polls opened two hours ago."

Spies are great at pretending, so we made believe that the bad part was over; we acted as if everything was going to be okay. We rolled down the windows and sang at the top of our lungs and tried not to think about why we had to make unscheduled stops, and turn without signaling, and dozens of other countersurveillance techniques that are the sign of really bad drivers and really good spies.

But no matter how good we were at vehicular counter-surveillance, there was at least one dangerous encounter that I knew we'd never outrun.

"We have her."

The truck stop was loud—full of the sounds of diesel engines and the clank of plates and silverware being cleared from greasy tables—and for a moment, I was afraid my mother hadn't heard me. "I said, we've got—"

"Yes, Professor Buckingham," Mom said slowly, and at first I started to correct her. I wanted to say that she'd mistaken the sound of my voice. Badly. But then Mom talked on. "It is *very* good to hear from you. In fact, I've been wondering *where you are now*, Patricia?" Mom asked, and I knew that someone was close.

"We're on our way to you," I said, not wanting to say too much over the phone. "Mom, I'm sorry we ran away." With every breath, the words came faster. "We tried to tell Madame Dabney, but everyone was so busy looking in Switzerland, but I just knew in my gut she wasn't there, and—"

"Of course things are ready for you here. If Macey has completed her biology test and is ready, the Secret Service should bring her here to D.C. so that she can join her parents *as soon as possible*."

I stepped farther down the narrow hallway, away from the crowded dining room, stretching the phone's greasy cord to its limit as I said, "They don't know she ran away, do they?"

"Of course not," Mom answered, the ultimate spy. "That's too much trouble."

I thought about Senator and Mrs. McHenry, and something made me smile.

"So how mad are they that she isn't there?"

"I've taken care of everything," Mom said, her voice still perfectly even and delightful.

A television blared live news coverage—a map of the United States, ready to be divided state by state into red and blue. It was election day in America, but there was one vote left that mattered, and, ironically, it was the one the McHenrys had lost a long time ago.

"Cam!" Bex yelled, "it's time."

"Mom," I said, suddenly needing to say it, "I love you."

A long pause filled the line. For a second, I thought I might have lost her.

"I feel exactly the same way. And Patricia." My mother's voice grew lower. "Hurry. And *be careful*."

I might have said a hundred other things, except the pay phone wasn't secure (not to mention sanitary), and besides, my friends—and our mission—were waiting.

The Operatives began preparations to go undercover inside hostile territory (a.k.a. the official Winters-McHenry presidential watch party).

Operatives Sutton and Baxter were thrilled to learn that this would require shopping for new clothes.

Unfortunately, according to Operative McHenry, to fully blend in, The Operatives' new clothes couldn't be too cute. Or comfortable.

Washington, D.C. was the first home I'd ever really known, but that night the streets felt foreign for the first time. Maybe it was the vehicle I was driving (Dodge mini-vans with state-of-the art engines aren't exactly common, you know), or maybe it was the fact that the most famous girl in the country was in the backseat in a red wig, but I felt anything but invisible as we turned down streets lined with news vans and Secret Service barricades.

As we walked closer to the hotel, we passed correspondents reporting live for every news outlet in the country, and I couldn't help myself—I thought about Boston. Beside me, Macey trembled, and I knew I wasn't the only one.

I was beginning to contemplate exactly how we were going to sweet-talk or sneak our way inside (Macey couldn't exactly show up Secret Service-less, after all!), when a familiar voice cut through the chaos. "Cameron!"

The Operatives remembered that potential kidnappers aren't always as scary as highly trained operatives-slash-mothers-slash-headmistresses who happen to know that you're away from campus without permission.

"Cammie," my mother called again, hurrying to meet us.

"Mom, I—" I started, wanting to explain or apologize, to beg forgiveness or mercy, but I didn't get to do any of that because, in the next instant, Secret Service agents swarmed around us. I noticed the comms unit in my mother's ear. I realized the agents around us were all women. One of the agents winked at me, and I wondered for a second if Aunt

Abby wasn't the only Gallagher Girl who had taken a special assignment.

And yet my mother didn't wink. She didn't smile. Instead, she grabbed my arm and steered us toward the building.

Something's happening, I thought. Something's wrong. There were a hundred questions I wanted to ask, but I didn't have the time—much less the breath—to do so as an emergency exit door was thrown open and my friends and I were ushered inside.

Walking through the narrow hallway, the sense of déjà vu was strong as we passed stacks of Winters-McHenry signs and catering carts—the backstage of the party—until finally we broke free into a space with gilded mirrors and silk-covered walls. It reminded me of Madame Dabney's tearoom and I realized that, in a way, our school had been preparing us for that moment for the past four and a half years.

A normal girl might have looked at the ornate ceilings and wondered if anything bad could ever happen in a place that beautiful. But we're Gallagher Girls. We know better.

"Macey," Mom said to my roommate, not even looking at me. "Go with these agents. Your parents are expecting you."

But Macey didn't move, and I remembered that this was the world Macey had been *born* into. The world she'd *chosen* was a shack by a lake.

"Go on, sweetheart," Mom urged.

Governor Winters himself passed by just then—and I knew we were in the middle of one of the most secure places in the country, and yet something hung in the air as my mother said, "I need to talk to Cammie a—"

I'm not sure what my mother would have said—what she would have told me—but she never had a chance to finish, because in the next instant a cry of "There you are" went through the room. The polls were closed, so maybe that's why Cynthia McHenry didn't hesitate to snap at her daughter. "What *are* you wearing?"

Macey reached up as if she'd forgotten all about the red wig.

"Protocol, ma'am," one of the agents at Macey's side replied. "We thought it best to keep your daughter disguised as we moved her from the school."

"Well, she's in a secure area now," Macey's mother said, then started through the ballroom, which was becoming fuller by the second. "Well, are you coming or not?" she asked, wheeling on us all. Macey looked at us as if asking for backup, but we knew that she had to go on alone.

She took a step away, but I was so busy trying to decipher the worry in my mother's eyes that I barely saw my friend move.

"Cam, we need—" Mom started, but again she didn't get to finish.

"Mrs. Morgan," Cynthia McHenry snapped. "Walk with me, please." Mom could have said no. She could have walked away.

But instead she said, "*Wait here*," and I knew she wasn't just my mother and headmistress—she was a Gallagher Girl, and she was going to cling to her cover to the end.

PROS AND CONS ABOUT CRASHING A
PRESIDENTIAL WATCH PARTY:

———

PRO: Secret Service personnel and members of the national media are everywhere, so your mother can't yell at you for running away.

CON: You know she will yell at you eventually, and the longer it builds up—the worse.

PRO: People who have given up sleeping, eating, and any kind of normalcy for two years (and/or vast amounts of money) in order to make someone president, really don't skimp on the giant shrimp for the food buffet.

CON: People who have been campaigning and living out of suitcases, buses, and trains for that amount of time also have a tendency to let their personal hygiene (not to mention their respect for personal space) get a little, shall we say, skewed.

PRO: It turns out, political watch parties come with bands!

CON: The bands play that same song from the campaign rallies over and over and over again.

———

Spies spend most of their time waiting. I know it sounds crazy, but it's true. And standing in that big ballroom that night, counting the balloons that hung in the nets overhead (there were are least 7,345, by the way), I couldn't help but think that we were experiencing the best covert operations training we've ever had.

Bex spent a good portion of the evening talking with an oil executive who we later learned was guilty of insider trading (a few days later we hacked into the Securities and Exchange Commission and left an anonymous tip, FYI). Liz used her photographic memory to reread her copy of *Advanced Encryption and You* in preparation for a big test in Mr. Mosckowitz's class.

But all I could do was think about the look in my mother's eyes as Cynthia McHenry pulled her away. I whispered, "Something's wrong."

"Cammie." A voice sliced through my worries, so I turned around. "Hey, I thought that was you," Preston said, making his way toward us.

Bex eyed him up and down. Liz fiddled with her top. At the front of the room, the announcer called everyone to silence, and ordered the sound on one of the televisions to be turned up while an anchorman said, "Yes, it's official. We are officially calling Ohio for Governor Winters and Senator McHenry."

A massive cheer filled the ballroom. People raised their glasses to toast the Buckeye state, but my mind was flashing back to the shadows beneath the bleachers on a sunny day.

"So, are you friends of Macey's too?" Preston asked, turning to Bex and Liz, and I could actually feel my grade in Culture and Assimilation take a nosedive.

"Oh, I'm sorry," I rushed to say. "Preston Winters, this is Rebecca."

"Bex," Bex corrected me in her American accent.

"And Liz," I said. Liz blushed but didn't say a word. "So, are you ready for this to be over?" I asked, because . . . well, I was pretty sure I was supposed to say *something*.

He looked around, then leaned closer and whispered, "Dying for it."

"I have a feeling the Secret Service wouldn't like your choice of words," Bex told him.

"I guess not." He laughed.

All around us I could feel the room changing as the night got later and the map on the wall became divided down the battle lines of red and blue.

"Hey," Preston said, looking at me. "Can I talk to you for a second?"

I glanced at Bex and Liz, who nodded for me to go, so the potential first son and I walked to a quiet corner of a party. "I fully admit that what I'm about to say will officially make me a girl." For a second, I forgot my fears and laughed. "And I'm owning that," the boy in front of me carried on. "So that's got to be worth something, right?"

"Right," I answered, biting back a smile.

"But it's just that I've got to ask you about . . . Does Macey ever *say* anything about me?" he finally blurted.

Despite my exceptional education, I totally didn't know how to answer his question. Maybe it was because we'd spent more than a year trying to figure boys out, but in all that time it had never crossed my mind that we might be just as encrypted to them. But more likely, it was because I didn't have a clue what to say.

"She doesn't say much about any of this," I finally admitted, gesturing around at the elaborate party—her other world. "It's not really . . . *her*, you know?"

Preston smiled. He did know. And right then I knew that it wasn't really him either.

"Do you ever think about Boston, Cammie?" he asked, but I didn't get a chance to admit that I did think about it—too much. "I do," Preston said, and then he smiled. "She's really something, isn't she?"

"Yeah," I said slowly. "She really is."

He looked at me then like I've been looked at maybe once or twice in my entire life, and I felt the subtle tremor that comes with being truly seen. "Something tells me she's not the only one."

"Preston—" I started, but the potential first son just shook his head.

"Whatever secrets you and Macey have, Cammie, I don't want to know them." He took a step away but then stopped suddenly and moved closer. "Just tell me one thing: does it involve Spandex?" He closed his eyes and a really goofy look crossed his face. "Because in my mind it involves Spandex."

"Preston," I said, laughing and slapping him gently on the arm.

I saw Macey walking toward Bex and Liz, and before I could say another word, Preston made a beeline toward her.

"Jeez, Preston." Macey rolled her eyes. "Don't you have a—"

"Macey," Preston said, cutting her off, "I came over to say that if our dads win, we're going to be seeing a lot of each other." Macey opened her mouth as if to protest, but Preston didn't let her draw a breath. "And if they lose . . . well, I think we still should see a lot of each other anyway. So there," he finished with a shrug. "That's all. You ladies enjoy the party."

And with that he walked away, and all Liz, Bex, Macey, and I could do was watch him go.

"Did he seem a little . . ." Macey started, but it was up to Bex and Liz to finish.

"Hot?" they said in unison.

Macey nodded like maybe it was true, maybe it was okay to admit it, maybe—just maybe—there might be an advantage to being the vice president's daughter after all. But then her gaze shifted and there was a sparkle in her eye. "And speaking of hot . . ." Macey said, "what's new with Zach?"

I thought about Preston, who had just done one of the bravest things I'd ever witnessed, and I realized that loving someone takes courage. It takes strength. But I'd never been brave when it came to Zach—I'd never taken the chance or said what I wanted to say. I thought of the way he'd looked at me at the football game, and it suddenly seemed too late.

"I don't think he likes me anymore. Maybe he never liked *me*. Maybe he just liked . . . *a challenge?*"

Macey shrugged. "It happens."

"No, Cam!" Liz protested. "Maybe he's just . . ." But she couldn't finish, because the only way that sentence could end was badly.

"Well, now's your chance to find out," Macey said as she pointed through the crowd at the boy who stood in its center with his hands in his pockets, his shoulders slumped as if he were the most harmless guy on earth.

"I heard someone's playing hooky," Zach told me. He smiled. Standing there, it felt almost like nothing bad had ever happened—or would ever happen again.

"There's a boy in my life," I told him. "He's a very bad influence."

Then Zach nodded. "Bad boys have a way of doing that. But they're worth it."

The ballroom was too hot and crowded. I felt almost dizzy as Zach leaned close to me and whispered, "Can I talk to you?"

As soon as I felt his hand in mine I forgot all about my mother's words. I didn't think about my promise. I wanted someplace quiet, someplace cool. And most of all, I wanted answers. So I let Zach lead me out a side door and onto a street that had somehow become an alley, thanks to Secret Service perimeters and D.C. blockades.

I shivered and wrapped my arms around my chest and wished I'd brought a winter coat. It suddenly seemed way too cold for the first Tuesday in November.

Someone had propped open a door to the hotel, and I heard the band stop. Some other state must have been called, because a moan rang through the night, but I wasn't really listening. Not anymore.

Because it was dark.

And I was cold.

And Zach was taking his jacket off and draping it around my shoulders, which (according to Liz, who double-checked with Macey) is the single-sexiest thing a guy can do.

His hands stayed on my shoulders a second longer than they had to. The jacket was warm and smelled like him. The wind blew harder, catching stray pieces of confetti in the breeze and whirling them around us like a patriotic snow-storm.

That was the moment when everything was supposed to be perfect.

After all, really cute boy? Check. Dramatic, romantic setting? Check. Close proximity without parental supervision? Double check.

But nothing about Zach is a regular boy, just like nothing about me is a regular girl, so instead, I looked at him and asked, "Why were you in Boston?"

Zach stepped back. He shook his head and looked down at the ground as he muttered, "There are things I can't tell you, Gallagher Girl."

"Can't?" I asked. "Or *won't?*"

But Zach didn't answer. He just looked at me as if to say, *What's the difference.*

"Tell me," I whispered, trying not to think about the fact that Zach wasn't chasing me anymore. Instead, he was staring down at me, and for the first time, I realized that he'd grown, that he was taller and stronger and not at all the boy who had kissed me last spring.

"There are some things you don't want to know."

I know it sounds crazy, but I believed him. After all, I've lived my whole life on a need-to-know basis, and right then I was willing to take Zach's word for it. I was willing to believe.

From the corner of my eye, I saw my roommates leave the hotel and step onto the street. I heard Macey call, "Cam!" But my gaze was locked with Zach's. Secrets and confetti lingered in the air around us until suddenly things grew dark and slow.

Until not knowing stopped being an option for me ever again.

Until I saw the van.

Chapter Twenty-Seven

I know it only lasted a few minutes. They've told me that. I've seen the surveillance video, what little there is. Still, the only thing I'm sure of is that one second we were standing in the shadows of the streetlamps, and the next, we were shrouded in black. Three city blocks were knocked out, and through the haze, only the Washington Monument kept shining.

"Macey!" I yelled, knowing more in my heart than in my mind that something was seriously wrong.

I started running down the street, away from Zach and toward my friend, just as headlights pierced the darkness, just as the barriers were crushed against the van that careened so quickly down the empty street that I actually stopped. I actually stared.

Macey. Macey had wandered closer to me and farther from Bex and Liz. She was there, standing alone in the headlights' glare, twenty yards from help of any kind.

"Run!" I yelled, rushing toward her, but it was too late. The van was too close. Its side door was sliding open. Masked figures were leaning out. Everything was so slow that I wasn't sure my yell would even reach her as she stood dumbfounded in the glare.

And watched the van pass her by.

We do these tests in CoveOps sometimes where Mr. Solomon asks us four or five different questions at once—some that make you process, some that make you recall, some that test your instincts, some that test your skill. And that's what it felt like. I know it sounds crazy. I know you won't believe me. But it really did feel like one of those tests as I stood in the light of the Washington Monument and memorized everything about the van; as I noted the type of wristwatch the driver was wearing, and whether or not the man jumping out the side door was likely to hit me first with his right hand or his left. As I thought about Boston; as I heard the words "get her" one more time; as I realized that Macey hadn't been the only Gallagher Girl on the roof that day.

As I remembered that nothing is ever as it seems.

Tires screeched across the pavement as the van skidded past me, turning ninety degrees, blocking off the path from which I'd come.

"Cammie!" Zach's yell seemed far away, lost behind a mountain of rubber and steel.

To my right, I saw my roommates running closer, but the

world was in slow motion. Help felt light-years away as a big man jumped from the back of the van. But he was too big—too slow. I dodged his blows and hooked my foot around the back of his knee as I pushed and he stumbled, pinning a second man against the van's door for a split second, and I started to run.

"Cammie!" Bex's voice rang through the night from the south.

"Macey!" I yelled in response. "Save Macey!"

But Macey didn't need saving. And I know now that *that* was the problem.

I didn't know what was happening. I didn't know where Zach had gone. All I knew was that I had to keep running—faster and faster until strong arms caught me around the waist. Before my feet even left the ground there was a rag over my mouth—a sick smell. I tried not to breathe as my arms flailed and the world began to spin.

And then falling.

I remember falling.

Through the eerie glow of the van's lights, I looked for Zach, but the figures were a blur as the pavement rushed up to meet me—too fast, too hard.

My head was on fire. My body was crushed beneath my attacker's weight. Someone or something must have knocked us both to the ground, because the rag was gone—the haze was parting just enough for me to see my roommates battling two men twice their size. Liz clung to the big man's back while Bex parried away his blows. Macey fought against the second man, and I wanted to yell for her to run, but my head throbbed as if there were simply too many facts—too many questions—for my mind to contain, and the words didn't come.

And then the crushing weight was gone. Clean air rushed into my lungs. But before I could push myself up, the rag was on my face again. The arms were gripping me tighter and the cloud over my eyes was growing thicker, so I summoned my last ounce of strength and crashed my head into my attacker's skull.

I heard a crack, felt the blood of a broken nose pouring over me as I stumbled to my feet. But the world was spinning too fast, my legs were too heavy. The arms found me again. I felt the van coming closer as my heels dragged against the pavement, and I searched the blurry darkness for help—for hope. And that's when I saw Macey.

She was running toward me. So strong. So fast. So beautiful.

"She's safe," I whispered, but no one heard the words—the lie.

I sensed the motion stop too late. I felt the right side of my body sinking, but I didn't fight to stand. Instead, I watched my roommate run faster, heard her call my name louder, but the one thought that filled my muddled mind was that the girl by the lake was no match for the girl in front of me then.

"No!" I heard the word but I didn't remember screaming. I saw the flash—heard the blast—but I hadn't seen the gun.

I lunged forward, but was too late. Not even the Gallagher Academy can teach someone to turn back time.

Yells filled the air. Panic spread on the wind as the gunshot echoed down the dark street and out into the night. And that's when I knew the voice I'd heard wasn't mine. Someone else was screaming. Someone else was running through the black. Someone else was lunging through the air in front of Macey and then falling too hard to the dark ground.

The hand with the gun tried to pull me back, but I spun and kicked, heard a sickening snap, and watched the masked figure fall.

I stepped, but my legs failed me. I fell to the ground and tried to crawl, but couldn't. Maybe it was the drugs from the rag, maybe it was the blow to my head, or maybe it was the sight of my roommate screaming over my aunt's broken body, but for some reason my arms forgot how to move.

"Get her out of here!" Mr. Solomon appeared as if from nowhere.

"Now!" My mother's voice echoed on the wind.

A hand grabbed my arm again, but this time I lashed out with more rage than I had ever felt, climbing to my knees, spinning, kicking, yelling, "Get . . ."

It was the eyes that made me stop. And the hands that were suddenly held toward me. And the words, "*Gallagher Girl.*"

I wanted to sink to the pavement, to rest. To sleep. But

Zach's hand found mine again. He pulled me to my feet as my head swam and my throat burned and the world went on crumbling all around me.

"Run," he said, dragging me back the way we'd come— north, toward the door of the hotel. Away from the van. Away from the fight. Away from the gunshot that still echoed through the darkest parts of my mind.

In the distance a siren wailed. Someone yelled, "United States Secret Service!" And forty feet away my aunt lay on the ground. Not moving.

Macey leaned over her. Zach's jacket had fallen from my shoulders, and Macey held it to the wound in Abby's chest, trying to stop the blood that spilled onto the dark asphalt, staining all it touched.

"Abby," I whispered, but Zach didn't let me pull away.

I heard the van come to life behind us. Secret Service agents yelled. More shots rang out, and yet I felt Zach stop. I ran into his shoulder, too busy looking behind me to see the man who stood between us and the door.

I saw the gun. I sensed the van as it rushed forward, seconds away and coming faster. I heard the screams of the fight behind us. But nothing that night was louder than the masked man's astonished whisper as he looked at the boy who stood beside me and said, "You?"

We have theories about what happened next—but no reasons. No *why*. Maybe it was the sirens or the Secret Service, but the man ran instead of fought. He fled into the darkness while my mother cried my name, but her voice was too high. Her momentum was too strong as she hurled her body against mine, driving me deep into the shadows.

A wall of bodies went up around me—Secret Service agents, police officers, the women who had escorted us from the van and into the hotel. The women who had been waiting . . . on me.

I tried to get up, but strong hands pushed me down, back against the building, safe underneath the walls of my sister-hood, which had been transported somehow from Roseville and were standing guard around me.

"Abby!" I cried as one of the women shifted. I could see through their legs to where my aunt lay on the ground, blood soaking her blouse, not moving. "Aunt Abby!" I yelled again.

My mind flashed back to Philadelphia. I saw an angel holding a fallen soldier, flying from the fires of war. "No!" I started to crawl like a child, weak and helpless, thinking about my father, who had died in a way I'll never know, in a place I'll never see, wondering in that terrible moment what was worse—not knowing, or watching the life seep out of someone you love before your very eyes.

My mother was screaming. She was falling to her knees at Abby's side. So I fought harder.

"Keep her down!" The voice was Mr. Solomon's. The tone was one I'd never heard before and I never hope to hear again. "They could come back!" The circle around me tightened. "They won't stop coming until they get her."

Get her.

All of my fight left me then. I fell against the wall while the sirens wailed and numbness came and the words echoed in the night.

Get me.

Chapter twenty-eight

2300 hours

"She's hysterical!" one of the paramedics said. The lights and sirens were too much for me. I yelled. I fought. I had to be heard.

"Give her something," a woman said.

"But—" the paramedic started.

"I'm her mother! Do it!"

0200 hours

"Doctors have no comment about the condition of the Secret Service agent who was shot last night in a reported drive-by shooting in downtown Washington, D.C. The agent had been assigned to Macey McHenry's personal detail, but reports indicate that, given the outcome of last night's election, Ms. McHenry will have no more need for protection from the Secret Service, that life for Macey McHenry can and will return to normal."

I heard the TV click off.

I stirred and blinked and recognized the room around me—the leather sofa, the shelves of books. But the drugs were too strong. Or maybe I was too weak.

I slept again.

0445 hours

"You girls should be in bed."

"No thank you, professor," Bex said.

"Rebecca, your mother and father have personally asked me to watch out for you, and I would like you to go to bed."

"I'm fine where I am, professor. Thank you."

"I had a feeling you might say that. At least let Ms. Sutton get some sleep."

0520 hours

I knew I wasn't alone. Bex's whispers were soft outside the door. Liz was mumbling something, half-asleep. Then a shadow cut across the room, and I saw Mr. Solomon standing in the moonlight, staring out across the grounds.

But it must have been the drugs—I must have still been sleeping—because it looked like his shoulders were shaking. I could have sworn his hand wiped across his face.

It wasn't real.

I was asleep.

Joe Solomon does not cry.

0625 hours

"Cammie." My mother's voice was high and scratchy, and I knew that she'd been crying. If you want to know the truth, that scared me most of all. I thought that maybe I was dead. I wondered if I was looking up from a coffin and not a leather couch. And then I thought about Aunt Abby.

"She's out of surgery," my mother said, answering my unasked question, reading my mind. She drew a deep breath. "She's out of surgery."

I pushed myself upright and a blanket fell from my lap to the floor. There were bandages on my head and arm. It was far too familiar to be anything but a very bad dream.

"Did you sleep, sweetheart?"

I thought it was an obvious question—a stupid waste of time. But all good interrogators know to start with the things the subject knows for sure. So I nodded my head. My mother said, "Good."

She was sitting on the coffee table in front of me—the very place where every Sunday night she laid out trays of veggies and bowls of dip. But that morning she just sat there with her hands in her lap. Was she a mother or a spy then? I'm not sure. But I knew the one I needed.

"Tell me," I demanded, not caring who heard—how far our voices carried. I saw Mr. Solomon by her desk, knew why he was there. "Both of you, start talking," I said, but Mom was easing toward me.

"Sweetheart, this is not something—"

"I have the right to know!"

She grew harder, still the boss of me and not about to let me forget it. "Cameron, there is a time and a place for—"

"They *weren't* after Macey," I said. "They were *never* after Macey. And . . . you knew."

"Cameron, this—" But Mom didn't get the chance to finish, because Mr. Solomon was easing onto the corner of her desk, crossing his arms as he said, "We didn't know anything more than you, Ms. Morgan. Not for a long time."

"But . . ." I started, my mind spinning, "Philadelphia." I thought about the closed door of my mother's office that next day, my aunt's newfound terror on the train. A chill like none I'd ever felt ran through me as I said, "What did Zach tell you in that tunnel, Mr. Solomon?"

My teacher nodded. He almost smiled. "He'd heard Macey wasn't the target. That was a possibility all along—we knew that, but Zach has sources—"

"What kind of sources? Who are they? Where are they? What—"

"That's all you get, Cammie," Joe Solomon said, and I hated him a little. But then he shrugged, defeated. "Because that's pretty much all there is."

Mr. Solomon is a good liar—the best. And I hated him for that too.

"Joe," my mom said calmly, as if I weren't ranting and

bruised. As if everything in my life weren't suddenly different. And over. "Could you give us a minute?"

A moment later, I heard the door open and close. I knew
we were alone.

"Sweetheart, don't . . ." She trailed off, unable to finish,
until the Gallagher Girl in her overruled the mother, and she
found the strength to carry on. "You're going to be okay,
Cammie. The Gallagher trustees have been notified. The full
strength of the school and The Agency are behind us. You're
going to be okay."

I love my mother's office. It's the closest thing to home
I've had in years. I sat there for a long time that morning
looking at the pictures that used to sit on her dresser in our
apartment in Arlington. Before she was a headmistress.
Before I was a Gallagher Girl. Before we lost Dad.

Before we lost a lot of things.

"What happens now?" I heard my voice crack and knew
that I was almost crying, almost pleading. My anger was
gone, and in its wake rushed a wave of grief and terror so
powerful that I could hardly breathe. I thought of Abby
bleeding. I thought of Macey and Preston. And finally, I saw
Zach as he hovered over me, as my mind whirled down a
laundry chute, plummeting in a free fall that I feared might
never end. "It's just . . . Mom . . . why?"

My mother held me. My headmistress smoothed my
hair. And the greatest spy I've ever known whispered, "We'll
find out. I promise we will find out."

Chapter twenty-nine

Classes should have ended, but they didn't. Finals week should have been over, but it was still weeks away. And yet every girl at my school knew that my roommates and I had already been tested. I thought about Aunt Abby, and I knew we'd barely passed.

It took three weeks for it to happen, for Mr. Solomon to knock on the door of Madame Dabney's tearoom, for my roommates and me to get called downstairs.

Following our teacher through the hall that day, I didn't let my mind wander—I knew too many dark places where it might go, so I kept my focus on the footsteps, on the stairs and on the walls. Until Mr. Solomon opened my mother's office door—

And someone said, "Hey, squirt."

"Abby!" Bex and Liz called at the same time, rushing toward her, throwing their arms around her.

"Girls," my mother said, as if to remind them that (at

least in Bex's case) they don't know their own strength.

My aunt was paler than I remembered. And thinner, almost frail. Her right arm was held in a sling. But her eyes were the same—so that's where I looked as I stepped closer.

"How are you?" I asked, almost afraid of the answer, but asking the question anyway.

My aunt smiled. "Never better." I wondered if she might be lying—or if I would be a good enough operative to know. "Evidently, Langley needs someone with a recent gunshot wound to impersonate a known arms dealer in . . . well . . . somewhere." She looked up at the sky and cocked her hip, then held her sling out for us to see. "Is this the ultimate cover or what?"

But, amazingly, the four of us didn't agree.

"Do you really have to go?" Liz glanced at Abby's suitcase. "You could stay here, couldn't you? You could teach?"

"Awesome!" Bex exclaimed, but Abby was already shaking her head, pulling her bag onto her good shoulder. But that didn't stop Bex from saying, "Ooh, you could come home with me for Christmas. Cam's coming. Mom and Dad would love to see you."

"Thanks, Bex," Aunt Abby said, "but I'm afraid I have some . . . *other* things I've got to do."

For about the millionth time in the past month I thought about what was happening outside our walls, but then I remembered not to ask the questions that I didn't want answered.

"So I guess I'll see you later." Abby hugged my mother,

who whispered something in her ear.

As she stepped toward the door she looked to my roommates and me. "Sorry, gang, but I don't do good-byes."

But then she stopped. She dropped her bag and turned. "Oh, what the heck."

And I can honestly say that none of the spy training in the world prepared me for the sight of my aunt grabbing Joe Solomon by the shirt.

And kissing him.

On the mouth.

For eighty-seven seconds.

Liz gasped. Bex stood there with her jaw on the ground. And me—I just looked at my mother, who was staring at the two of them as if her world couldn't possibly get any weirder.

When it was over, Aunt Abby finally came up for air (Mr. Solomon, I noticed, didn't do much of anything). My aunt looked at her sister, cocked a hip, and said, "Well, someone had to do it."

And that was when she walked away.

Mom and Mr. Solomon were still pretty dumbfounded, given what had just transpired and all, but Bex, Macey, Liz, and I chased after her, watching the living legend who shares my name walk through the Hall of History, past the sword that had started it all, and then start down the Grand Staircase, away from us.

In that one final second, everyone I loved was warm and safe.

"Don't be a ghost this time." My voice sliced through

the empty foyer. "Go do what you have to do, but don't be a ghost, okay?"

Abby turned to me, then pulled a jacket from the bag on her shoulder. "Here. I think someone gave this to you."

I didn't look to see if my aunt's blood still stained Zach's jacket. I didn't let myself think about that night. Instead, I just took it and tried to think about why he had given it to me and nothing else.

"Abby." It was Macey's voice, and by the look on her face, she was as shocked as anyone to hear it. "I never said . . . I mean, you should know . . . I guess what I'm trying to say is . . ."

Abby stopped. Her good hand was on the smooth banister. Her hair fell over one shoulder as she smiled, slipped on her regulation sunglasses, and said, "I told you I'd take a bullet for you."

And then she walked away.

I stood there for a long time, watching her go, because that's all that was left to do.

Bex and Macey went into the Grand Hall for lunch. Liz walked to the library. I stood alone, telling myself that my aunt would come back someday—that the world needed her outside the walls of my school, and for the time being, I was needed inside.

That for the time being, all I could do was wait.

"Seventh grade!" Patricia Buckingham's voice carried through the foyer as the newest Gallagher Girls followed behind her, out of the Grand Hall. "We will proceed in a group to the lab for your examination. Do not enter until I have given you your—" She stopped suddenly and yelled to the girls at the front of the pack, "Emily Sampson! I saw that!"

I wondered if I had ever been that small. I saw the innocence in their eyes, and I knew somehow that I would never feel that way again. I'd seen too much—I knew too little. And for reasons I didn't even know at the time, I raced after them.

"Professor Buckingham," I called, stepping closer to the woman who was both the oldest member of the Gallagher Academy faculty and also the only member whose appearance hadn't changed at all since I was in the seventh grade.

"Yes, Cameron?" Buckingham said, and in that moment she seemed timeless. As if some great twentieth-century spymaster had carved her out of stone.

"I have a question . . . about history."

"History of Espionage is a course on the spring semester curriculum, Cameron. I expect you to know that." She ushered another seventh grader down the long hall. "Right now, as you can see, I am quite busy helping our newest students acclimate. Sissy!" Buckingham yelled as she pushed them along, farther from me, while the wind howled louder outside.

"Yes, ma'am," I said. "I can see that. It's just that I was wondering . . . about the Circle of Cavan." When she turned, her blue eyes pierced into mine.

"I need to know . . ." I called after her, my voice

cracking under the weight of the fears that I'd been carrying for weeks. "I need to be ready."

"I'm sorry, Cameron. It's not something . . . I'm sorry." She took a step. The voices of the seventh graders faded away as they turned the corner—disappeared from sight.

I turned to stare out the windows, watched the first flakes of winter start to fall and blow across the grounds. In a few hours, everything would be covered, as if the earth itself were pulling on its best disguise.

"Perhaps in the spring." Buckingham's voice cut through the drafty corridor, chasing after me like a strong wind. I turned to look at her. "Yes," she said again, and for a split second—nothing more—she looked like an old woman. The hallway felt like time itself, and Patricia Buckingham and I were standing at opposite ends—her looking back on all she'd seen, me wondering what lay ahead.

Then Professor Buckingham nodded once more and said softly, "Perhaps in the spring."

I watched her disappear down that long corridor while outside the sky turned gray and the ground turned white and winter settled in.

Zach's jacket was in my arms, so I put it around my shoulders. It hung there, heavy and warm, and the cold seemed a little farther away. As I put my hands in the pockets, I felt something brush against my fingers. I pulled out a small piece of Evapopaper and studied the handwriting I'd seen twice before:

Have fun in London

-Z

And then, despite everything, I smiled and looked at the note and knew that spring would come—it always does. So I stared out that cold window, watching my breath collect on the glass, trying not to think about my life after the thaw.

PROS AND CONS ABOUT WRITING THE GALLAGHER GIRLS SERIES: A LIST BY ALLY CARTER

Pro: You get to have the most amazing readers in the world.

Con: Unfortunately, trying to write books worthy of those readers takes time. I'm incredibly grateful to everyone who has waited so patiently.

Pro: Working with all of the talented people at Disney • Hyperion Books is a phenomenal blessing. I owe so much to everyone there, especially the amazing Jennifer Besser, who took me in when I had no home. Jen, the best is yet to come!

Con: Writing is a solitary business. I don't know how I'd make it without the support and encouragement of writers like Maggie Marr and Jennifer Lynn Barnes, who read this book in its earliest and roughest form. And, of course, the BOBs.

Pro: You get to have Kristin Nelson as your agent.

Con: It's difficult to visit all places the Gallagher Girls

have to go, so I offer my heartfelt apologies to the people of Boston, Cleveland, and Philadelphia for the liberties I took when describing their fair cities.

Pro: It's so much easier to write about loving parents and loyal sisters when you have personal examples you can draw from. So most of all, I thank my family.